MIRAGE CHASER: DESERT DREAM

Love, Danger, and the Unseen

ECHO SABLE

TABLE OF CONTENTS

CHAPTER 1

CHASING AN ILLUSION

The rain hammered relentlessly against the windowpanes, each drop a tiny messenger heralding the unexpected. Hidden away in my study, I was ensnared by a malaise of monotony when the doorbell's chime shattered the quiet, a sound as startling as a lighthouse beam slicing through fog. The servant's footsteps echoed down the hallway, and soon, standing in the foyer, was Mateo —a man whose life on the seas was as enigmatic as the treasures he brought from distant lands.

Years had passed since Mateo first embarked on his maritime journey after graduating from the Navigation School. Aboard a leviathan of an oil tanker, he had ascended the ranks with the precision of a well-calibrated sextant. From trainee third mate to second mate, and finally to first mate at the tender age of thirty-two, his career unfolded like a sailor's map, each promotion a waypoint etched in the annals of his seafaring saga.

In the years before, our meetings were as regular as the tides, every six months like clockwork. His vessel, a behemoth gliding through the Middle East's azure waters, would dock near my city, and Mateo would arrive, arms laden with exotic trifles from lands kissed by the sun. Our conversations spanned the globe, from bustling bazaars to tranquil deserts, and his tales were rich with the scents and sounds of places far from the mundane.

Mateo was a navigator by nature, his soul attuned to the siren call of the open sea. Yet, he was equally at ease traversing the variegated tapestry of the land, his footprints marking many a Middle Eastern country.

But the world had shifted; the Suez Canal lay closed, and now his tanker, no longer taking shortcuts, swept around the Cape of Good Hope. The sea voyage stretched interminably, prolonging his absence into a span of a year and a half.

That rain-soaked afternoon, Mateo's appearance at my door was a welcome surprise, a balm to my dulled senses. "Mateo, come up quickly!" I called, my voice echoing down the stairs as rain streamed from his raincoat like rivulets carving paths through stone. He ascended, cradling a mysterious wooden box—a foot square—as if it held the secrets of the ocean itself. Despite his smile, there was a flicker in his eyes, a shadow whispering of unspoken burdens.

We met midway on the stairs, sharing a brief moment of camaraderie in a world of shifting sands, before retreating into the warmth of the study. As he set the box down, I tapped its lid with curiosity. "What strange thing did you bring me this time?" I asked, my words a playful challenge as ancient as the mariner's call to adventure.

Mateo's smile was enigmatic as he carefully lifted the lid of the wooden box, revealing an ancient and peculiar relic—a crocodile mummy. "This," he said, his voice tinged with mystery, "was stolen from the pyramid of an Egyptian Pharaoh. The Egyptians claim it wards off evil spirits."

Though crocodile mummies weren't exactly my personal interest, the artifact's exotic origin commanded a certain respect. After a moment's admiration, I set it aside, and our conversation resumed amidst the relentless downpour. Yet, Mateo's demeanor was off, his usual vibrancy dimmed. Initially, I dismissed it as my own over-sensitivity, but soon it became clear he was harboring a secret.

"Mateo," I ventured, "is there something special you'd like to discuss?"

Staring out at the rain-swept world beyond the window, Mateo confessed, "Yes, I'm in love."

I couldn't help but chuckle. Mateo, the eternal wanderer, in love? It was a revelation worthy of headlines, especially from a man who had once claimed that those who roamed the world had no need for a home.

I had often teased him about what he would do if he ever found himself in love. Mateo had boasted that no woman existed who could ensnare his heart. Yet here he was, entangled in the very emotion he had deemed improbable, and it was clear his heart was troubled by it.

"That's wonderful," I teased. "You're nearly forty. Isn't it about time you fell in love?"

As he spoke of his newfound affection, a particular glow brightened his eyes, a stark contrast to the melancholy shadow on his face. His spirits, however, were undeniably lifted. "Would you like to see her photo?" he asked, a hint of pride in his voice.

I knew without needing to see it that the "her" he mentioned was someone extraordinary, for it would take an exceptional woman to captivate a man like Mateo.

With a nod, I watched as he solemnly retrieved a slim, elegant photo album from his coat pocket. The album, though no larger than a postcard, was a work of art—bound in camel skin with silver-inlaid corners.

Its exquisite craftsmanship spoke volumes of how precious the contents were to him. Handing it to me, Mateo explained, "I have four photos of her in total."

In that moment, as the rain played its symphony outside, the room was charged with the anticipation of unveiling a piece of Mateo's heart—a new puzzle in the ever-turning labyrinth of life.

I opened the album, realizing it was designed to hold only four precious photos. The first image was a grainy black-and-white shot, marred by the imperfections of rudimentary photography.

In the frame stood several palm trees, stark sentinels of the desert, framing a small oasis. Beside the pool, a group of women were gathered, two balancing water jars atop their heads with practiced grace.

One woman, however, caught my eye. She was crouched by the water's edge, her head turned slightly to glance back. Though her face was obscured by a veil, her eyes shone with an almost ethereal brightness.

Though I kept silent, my mind buzzed with questions. Mateo, a man of discernment and taste, had only four photos of his beloved. Surely, they should be carefully composed masterpieces. So why lead with such a blurry image?

Three Arab women occupied the scene. Which one was the object of his affection?

I looked up, questioning Mateo with a glance.

He anticipated my unspoken query, pointing to the woman by the pool. "That's her," he confirmed.

I frowned slightly. "Did you take this photo?"

Mateo nodded, a hint of sheepishness in his expression. "Yes, I did."

I shook my head, teasing lightly, "Your photography skills leave much to be desired."

Mateo gave a rueful smile. "I had no choice, but the next three photos—they're miraculously clear."

His words piqued my curiosity, the phrases "no choice" and "miraculously clear" shrouded in mystery.

I turned the page, and upon seeing the second photo, a gasp escaped my lips.

The second image was indeed a revelation—a striking contrast to the first, vivid and sharp, as if the woman in the photo might step from the page at any moment.

The second photo seemed to have been captured mere moments after the first. The Arab girl still held her pose, her gaze cast backward. Those large, liquid eyes were arresting, capable of ensnaring any observer in a momentary reverie, compelling them to utter a silent, awestruck, "So beautiful."

Her smile was enchanting, a sweetness that seemed almost tangible. A few wisps of her long hair danced across her face, enhancing her allure.

I had always known that anyone who could capture Mateo's heart would be extraordinary, and here was the proof before me.

"How did you meet her?" I asked, curious about the story behind the photograph.

Mateo, lost in admiration, replied, "She is truly beautiful, isn't she?"

I nodded in agreement. "No one could argue with that."

As I turned to the third page, the transformation was clear. The girl had risen to her full height, tall and elegant, her grace amplified, her smile still radiant.

The fourth photo captured her with a water jar balanced effortlessly on her head, her smile even more dazzling.

I pointed to the image. "Mateo, when a girl smiles at you like that, it seems your pursuits might not be in vain. Yet, you seem troubled. Is it because Muslims are reluctant to marry foreigners?"

Mateo's smile turned wry. "That's a concern far in the future. The problem you mention is not even on the horizon."

I was taken aback. "What do you mean? You haven't even approached her? Surely, with a smile like that..."

His expression grew pained. "You're mistaken. She wasn't smiling at me."

A frown creased my brow. "Oh. So this photo wasn't taken by you? Do you have a rival?"

Mateo shook his head. "No, I took the photo."

Confused, I studied the image again. "Then I don't understand. If you took the photo, surely she was smiling at you. What's her name? Arab names can be tricky to remember."

Rising, Mateo spread his hands in defeat. "Her name? I don't even know her."

Stunned, I realized his narrative was unraveling into something beyond my comprehension.

He continued, his demeanor distant, his words tangled with an underlying tension. "I have seen her and captured her in my photos, yet she has never seen me."

I stared at him, my mind grappling with the paradox. Despite my efforts, I couldn't decipher Mateo's cryptic revelation.

After a moment of contemplation, a revelation struck me. "Oh!" I exclaimed. "You took the photo secretly! But if you're so captivated by her, why not just find her and talk to her?"

Mateo shook his head again, his frustration palpable. "I would love to, but I have no idea where she is."

His words only deepened my confusion, and impatience bubbled up inside me. I tapped the table for emphasis. "What are you talking about? I think even you don't grasp it fully, so how could I?"

Mateo sighed, resigned. "I understand it perfectly."

"Then spell it out clearly," I insisted. "Stop being cryptic and evasive."

Nodding, he continued, "You know my passion for travel. One day, our ship docked at a port, giving me three days of rest. I stocked up on water and food, rented a jeep, and set off into the desert. I'd heard tales of ancient submerged cities hidden in the sands and wanted to explore."

I interrupted, eager for answers. "And that's when you stumbled upon this romance and met the Arab girl?"

"You could say that," Mateo replied, "but it's far more complicated than you think."

I studied him, exasperated by his hesitance. Few things are more irritating than a story told with unnecessary vagueness, and he was testing the limits of my patience.

I folded my arms, waiting for him to unravel his tale. He sighed again, meeting my gaze, and said, "Here's what happened. After driving about ten miles into the desert, I suddenly spotted an oasis ahead— teeming with people, palm trees, and pools."

I couldn't resist interjecting, "Every oasis has those. Spare me the details."

Sensing my impatience, Mateo spread his hands helplessly. "But she wasn't at any other oasis."

Realization dawned. "You're saying she's the ideal you're fixated on?"

"Yes, exactly. Hear me out," he implored. "I saw this oasis and drove toward it. But no matter how far I drove, it remained just out of reach, always half a mile away. Do you understand?"

A light bulb went off in my mind. "Ah," I gasped, "it's a mirage!"

Mateo nodded vigorously. "Exactly!"

The concept of a mirage, while easily explained by optical science, never failed to intrigue me. It was a phenomenon as elusive and captivating as Mateo's narrative—something not everyone traveling the desert experiences.

Eager to hear more, I urged him, "Go on!"

Mateo's story continued with an intensity that matched his fascination. "It's not my first time in the desert," he explained, "but encountering a mirage was a first for me. Once I realized what it was, I stopped the car and used a telescope to observe what lay ahead. Through the lens, I could see everyone clearly, as if they were right in front of me."

"That's truly intriguing," I noted. "You can see them, yet their actual location eludes you."

"Exactly!" Mateo's excitement was palpable. "I was thrilled. After a while of observing, I took several photos with a telephoto lens."

The revelation made me catch my breath, adding another layer to the mystery of Mateo's infatuation.

He shrugged, "And that's how it happened."

I pressed him, "What do you mean, 'that's how it happened'? You said you fell in love with the Arab girl—how did that feeling take root?"

Mateo frowned, "When I was photographing her, I thought she was strikingly beautiful. The image left a profound mark on my mind. But it wasn't until I developed the photos that I realized how much I was drawn to her."

His expression was earnest, his eyes reflecting a depth of feeling that was unmistakable. Yet, who was he truly in love with? An Arab girl he had never met—except through the ephemeral vision of a mirage. It seemed an unattainable, almost illusory affection.

Standing, I placed a comforting hand on his shoulder, treating him with the care one might offer a younger brother. "Let it go, Mateo. It's not love in the traditional sense. This is something too intangible."

Mateo looked up, his eyes searching. "Ash, if a mirage shows a place, it must exist somewhere in reality, right?"

"Indeed. A mirage is essentially a refraction of light."

"Then," Mateo's voice was firm, "there must be such a person for me to have seen her and captured her photo."

"You could argue that," I conceded.

His face lit up with a renewed determination. "Exactly! If she exists, then I can find her!"

I was momentarily speechless. Mateo's logic was compelling. The girl he saw, while a product of refracted light, had to have a real counterpart. After all, a mirage, though a virtual image, relies on a real entity to form. His belief, though rooted in the extraordinary, was grounded in a truth that I could not deny.

Despite Mateo's conviction, I struggled to share his optimism. The mirage had appeared half a mile away, but the actual location of the entity could be a thousand miles distant. The odds of finding her seemed insurmountable.

I slowly shook my head, but Mateo's excitement only grew. "Since she exists, my love isn't just a fantasy. I just need to find her," he insisted.

Though I didn't want to dampen his spirits, I had to inject some realism. "Mateo, you have to realize you might never find her."

Mateo's smile was tinged with bitterness, acknowledging the truth in my words. "That's why I need your help," he implored.

I chuckled, trying to lighten the mood. "How am I supposed to help with something so outlandish? No one knows where your mystery woman is!"

But Mateo was earnest. "You've traveled extensively. I'm asking you to examine the photo closely."

I sighed. "I've studied it, Mateo. Honestly, there's nothing unique about it. Every small Arab village looks like that."

Quiet fell between us. "And there are countless villages like that across the Arab world. It's an impossible task," I added.

Mateo fell silent, contemplative. After a moment, he pulled a map from his belongings, spreading it on the table. He pointed to a red cross. "This is where I saw the mirage."

His finger rested on a spot west of Oman, on the edge of the Rub' al Khali Desert.

Mateo gazed at the map, his finger resting on the vast expanse of the Sande Desert. "This desert is also called the Sande Desert," he mused. "Sandy is a fitting name for a girl, so I've named my mystery beauty Sandy."

I couldn't suppress a chuckle. "Alright, your Sandy. You've glimpsed her there, but what's the point? What you saw was just an illusion."

Undeterred, Mateo pressed on. "I want to know if it's possible to calculate the distance between the entity and the mirage based on the location where I saw it. At least to figure out the direction?"

I shook my head, bemused by the complexity of his ambition. "Mateo, if you could manage that, you'd not only find your Sandy but also secure a Nobel Prize!"

The exchange hung in the air, a blend of humor and the tantalizing allure of an unsolved mystery. Mateo's quest for Sandy—an intersection of science, faith, and yearning—was both an extraordinary pursuit and a testament to the human spirit's boundless curiosity.

CHAPTER 2

DESPERATE SEARCH

Mateo's face was etched with a deep, haunting pain as he stared at the sprawling map. I traced a finger over the vast expanse. "Look, the Sandy Desert stretches a thousand kilometers wide and seven hundred kilometers long. This elusive village could be anywhere within these 700,000 square kilometers. Or it might lie beyond, across the Gulf of Oman in Iran, or even further afield in Pakistan or Saudi Arabia, perhaps Yemen. This search is a daunting task."

He listened intently, absorbing my words, and when I finished, his resolve was unshaken. "Ash, I can't just let it go. I've resigned from my position. I've decided to dedicate my life to finding Sandy!" His declaration left me stunned. Mateo had ascended to a commendable rank on the tanker, with prospects for even higher advancement. Yet, he had chosen to forsake it all for a phantom love.

I couldn't help but see the romance in his decision, something straight out of poetry or novels, but it was a reality that bewildered me. "You must be joking!" I exclaimed.

"Not at all," he replied with a serene determination. "I'll depart tomorrow on my final voyage to the Middle East. From there, I'll wander the desert until I find Sandy."

I raised my voice in desperation. "You'll never find Sandy, only the sands of the Sande Desert!"

His calm response was unwavering. "Even knowing that, I must try. I've fallen in love with Sandy, and without her, everything else is meaningless."

His conviction was unyielding, leaving me at a loss for words. "Well, then," I finally said, "I wish you the best of luck. Since you're leaving tomorrow, let me treat you to dinner tonight."

Mateo shook his head. "I don't need a dinner. I need your help."

"You know it's not that I don't want to help," I replied, feeling helpless. "It's just that I don't know how."

"You know a lot of people—scholars, experts on mirages—someone who might offer guidance."

I sighed, resigned. "Alright, I'll reach out to them for you."

He continued with a hint of frustration, "Once I reach Oman, I'll try to keep in touch. Alas, the villages are so isolated. If only people read newspapers there, I could publish Sandy's photo in hopes that she'd see it."

The enormity of his quest weighed heavily on us both, a search driven by love and the hope of turning an illusion into reality.

A sudden thought struck me, and I couldn't help but voice it. "Mateo, have you considered that your Sandy might already have a husband and children? Even if you find her, it might be pointless."

I hoped these words would make him reconsider the arduous path he was about to take. But Mateo, unwavering in his conviction, replied, "No, no. Look at the photos—only a young virgin girl can smile with such innocence."

They say that reason abandons those in love, and Mateo was the perfect embodiment of this adage.

He carefully folded the map and tucked the photos back into his jacket pocket with a solemnity that spoke volumes. "Goodbye," he said, a touch of melancholy in his voice.

I felt a pang of sadness, knowing his quest was fraught with uncertainty. "I wish you good luck," I repeated, though the words felt inadequate.

As Mateo disappeared into the rain, I stood at the door, watching him fade into the downpour, a lone figure against a world of uncertainty.

Back in my study, I spent hours poring over books on mirages, yet none could offer insight into the phenomenon that had ensnared Mateo's heart.

When Flora returned that evening, I recounted the story of Mateo's quixotic pursuit.

Women, at times, possess a unique brand of logic, and Flora was no exception. "Ah, so romantic," she sighed. "We should do everything in our power to help him."

I replied with a hint of sarcasm, "Sure, we could wander the desert like him. That would triple his chances of finding Sandy."

Flora frowned, unimpressed by my cynicism. "You shouldn't make fun of him. There must be another way to help."

I offered a smile. "If you have any good ideas, I'm listening."

After a moment's thought, Flora proposed, "What if we photocopy Sandy's photo and distribute hundreds of thousands through our friends in Arabia, reaching every village?"

I was taken aback. Initially, I had expected to dismiss her suggestion with a laugh, certain that finding the woman Mateo called "Sandy" was an impossible task. But Flora's idea, while ambitious, had merit.

While it was unlikely that our network could reach every village in the vast Arab region, I knew several influential friends who could make a significant impact. Even if we reached just a tenth of the villages, it would give Mateo a fighting chance.

Realizing the potential of her plan, I sprang to my feet. "You're right, Darling. I'll find him."

"Do you know where he is?" she asked.

"I can find out," I assured her.

"Then hurry," Flora urged. "If Mateo find her, it will be such a beautiful love story."

I smiled, feeling a renewed sense of purpose. "It would indeed be very touching."

Flora handed me a raincoat, and as the rain poured down, I dashed out into the storm. Half an hour later, I arrived at the shipping company and discovered that Mateo was staying at the senior seamen's club. When I reached his room, the waiter informed me he was down in the bar located in the cellar.

I hurried down to the bar, and as I approached the entrance, I was met with the sounds of chaos—shouting and fighting, as if a full-blown brawl had erupted. Several people were rushing out, and one nearly collided with me. I grabbed him, asking, "What's happening in there?"

He managed to gasp out, "Fighting."

Pushing past him, I entered the dimly lit bar, which was now in shambles. I shouldered my way through a throng of people and spotted Mateo, engaged in a fierce fight. He landed a powerful punch on a burly man, sending him reeling.

I called out, "Mateo!"

My shout distracted him at a critical moment. He turned to see who had called his name, unable to dodge the incoming blow—a wine bottle smashed against the back of his head. The bottle shattered, and the wine mixed with blood, painting his face red. He staggered and began to fall.

Before he hit the floor, I shoved aside three men who were charging at me. The combatants in the bar were inebriated, but I was stone-cold sober, giving me the upper hand.

I reached Mateo just in time, grabbing his arms and dragging him out. As we made our way to the bathroom, I had to fend off more attackers, knocking four of them out cold.

Once in the bathroom, I thrust Mateo's head into the wash basin and doused him with cold water for half a minute. The sound of a police siren drew nearer, prompting me to hurry. I hauled him out of the bathroom and, supporting him, we ascended the back stairs.

Mateo clutched his head, groaning in pain. I helped him into his room, where he collapsed onto the floor with a heavy thud.

He struggled to his feet, and I refrained from assisting him, observing as he wobbled to a standing position. His eyes, wide and unfocused, met mine, and for a moment, I doubted whether he recognized me, so disoriented he appeared.

After what seemed like an eternity, Mateo finally recognized me. "It's you," he said, his voice tinged with surprise. "What are you doing here?"

"I came to find you," I replied, my tone steady and purposeful.

He sank into the sofa, exhaustion evident in his posture. "What's the matter?" he asked.

"Mateo," I began, my voice firm, "someone like you isn't meant for brawling."

Mateo attempted to spring to his feet, but his energy faltered, and he slumped back into the sofa. His eyes were wide with indignation. "Two guys mocked me, called me a fool, said I was being deceived. How could I not fight back?"

I frowned, trying to piece together the puzzle. "Why did they mock you?"

He lowered his head, shame and frustration mingling in his expression. "I was at the bar, drinking, staring at Sandy's photo. A man next to me struck up a conversation, and I told him how I captured Sandy's image."

"Did he laugh at you?" I inquired, seeking clarity.

"No," Mateo replied, his voice tinged with bitterness. "He listened intently. Then, after I finished, he patted my shoulder and offered to find Sandy for me—for a price. He claimed all it would take was a thousand dollars."

I couldn't help but draw a sharp breath upon hearing Mateo's tale, anticipating the inevitable conclusion. As expected, he continued, his speech still slurred from the alcohol, yet earnest in his recounting.

"What's a thousand dollars?" he exclaimed. "If it means finding Sandy, I handed it over without hesitation. I even gave him Sandy's photo. But once he left, two guys started poking their noses in, telling me I'd been duped. That's when the fight broke out."

I sighed deeply. "Mateo, do you still believe you weren't tricked?"

Mateo's eyes bore into mine, a challenge flickering within them. For a moment, it seemed as if he might lash out again, and I braced myself, ready to defend against his anger. But instead, he held back, his gaze softening, a bitter smile tugging at his lips. "Perhaps I was fooled," he admitted, "but as long as there's a glimmer of hope, I can't let it slip away."

His words weighed heavily on me, mixing pity with a touch of admiration. Mateo wasn't naive. Even in his drunken state, he wouldn't easily trust a stranger with a thousand dollars. He understood the risk, but he was willing to pay for a flicker of hope, however remote.

The fight with those meddling men was sparked by that fragile hope. They had shattered his illusion, and in doing so, they had struck at the core of his desperate yearning. His reaction was one of deep-seated sorrow and frustration.

I placed a hand on his shoulder, my voice gentle yet probing. "Mateo, do you truly love this Arab girl that much?"

He nodded, a rueful smile playing on his lips. "Yes, I know it's irrational, a path fraught with heartache, but I can't quell these feelings."

Until now, I'd found his story amusing, something to chuckle over in disbelief. But at this moment, my amusement faded, replaced by a solemn resolve. My voice took on a serious tone, as if I were making a vow.

"In that case, Mateo, I'll do everything in my power to help you find her," I pledged, recognizing the gravity of his longing and the depth of his commitment.

Mateo must have sensed the affirmation, sincerity, and determination in my words, and he gripped my hand tightly, repeating, "Thank you, thank you so much!" His gratitude was palpable, and I could see how much my promise meant to him.

"The first step," I said, "is to make many copies of her photos."

"That's easy," Mateo replied, reaching for a box. He handed me an envelope containing the negatives. "I'll give you these."

I continued, "I'll leave before you to make arrangements. Then, when your ship arrives, we can meet up."

Mateo nodded, "Alright. The tanker will dock at Shur Port in Oman, and I'll meet you there."

"Okay," I agreed.

I wanted to say, "I hope we'll have everything figured out by the time we meet at Shur Port," but I held back. This wasn't a joke to him, and raising his hopes only to dash them later would be cruel.

We shook hands, and I advised Mateo to get some rest. With the negatives in hand, I headed home.

That night, I worked late into the night, developing two clear photos from the four negatives in my darkroom. When I enlarged them, Flora glanced at the images and gasped, "This Arab girl is so beautiful. No wonder Mateo is captivated by her."

I smiled, knowing the journey ahead. "I've promised Mateo I'll find her. We might be apart for half a year or even a year."

"If you can find this girl for Mateo, it will be worth it," Flora said with a smile. "Besides, you can always reach out, and I can join you anytime."

"Of course," I agreed. "We've traveled to many places together, but we've never explored Arabia."

I stifled a yawn, and Flora chuckled, "You should get some sleep. There's plenty to do tomorrow."

The following days were a whirlwind of activity. I managed travel arrangements and contacted my Arab friends in advance. Three days later, I set off on my journey.

Upon arriving at the port of Aden, my schedule intensified. I visited each friend I knew, scouring the areas under their jurisdiction for any sign of the Arab girl.

Naturally, many people were curious about my mission, prompting me to share the fabricated story I had prepared. I carefully omitted any mention of the mirage, crafting a more believable tale instead. Some friends even jested, "Who is she? An Israeli spy, perhaps?" I had to laugh along and explain my story yet again.

After a whirlwind of activity, I finally arrived at Shur Port. Mateo had gotten there a day before me. Shur Port was a modest place, with only one hotel that boasted decent facilities. As soon as I stepped inside, Mateo spotted me.

At first, I didn't recognize him. It had been less than a month since we'd parted, but in that short time, his transformation was shocking.

He had shed at least 20 pounds. Once a handsome man, he now appeared gaunt and worn. His eyes were hollow, his skin had darkened, and a vitality seemed to have left him. When he stood to greet me, I was momentarily stunned before I called out, "Mateo!"

Mateo shuffled towards me, his movements unsteady, almost spectral. I couldn't bear to see him struggle, so I rushed forward to meet him, taking hold of his arm. "Mateo, are you alright?"

"Me?" he replied with a bitter smile, touching his cheek. "I've lost a lot of weight, haven't I?"

"You're not just thin, Mateo; you seem distant. What's happened?"

His smile only grew more pained. "You know why I'm here. I haven't slept well. Every time I close my eyes, I see her."

His confession left me with a heavy heart. I knew he was captivated by the girl, but I hadn't realized the depth of his obsession. If this kept up, if the Arab girl remained elusive for another three months, Mateo might waste away entirely. His current state was a living embodiment of the word "emaciated."

I chose not to press further, instead shaking his hand. He said, "I've rented a double room for us."

"Alright," I agreed. "I have a lot to discuss with you."

Once in the room, I recounted all the efforts I had made since arriving in Arabia. Hearing about my endeavors seemed to lift Mateo's spirits somewhat.

I added, "I also consulted experts. They mentioned that most mirages are inverted reflections."

Mateo shook his head emphatically. "No, what I saw wasn't a reflection. Those people appeared so vividly, as if they stood right before me, not mere reflections but real presences."

I continued, "If it's an inverted reflection, the virtual image of a mirage is usually not too far from the real object because it forms after a single refraction. But if not, with multiple refractions, the reflection can be much farther, even spanning oceans."

Mateo stared at me, his expression blank and lost. "Then where is she?" he asked, his voice tinged with desperation.

Sympathy welled up in me; I couldn't bring myself to crush his hopes completely. Still, the odds of finding such a girl were slim. I tried a gentle approach. "Mateo, if you have an affinity for Arab girls, I know a tribal chief with three daughters, each as beautiful as a tale from Arabian Nights—"

Before I could finish, Mateo shot up, his voice sharp and commanding, "Shut up!" His chest heaved with emotion, and his gaunt frame only amplified the intensity of his reaction.

"If we weren't good friends," he said after a moment, "I might have hit you." I realized then that pushing him further could be dangerous. I managed a smile and said, "Let's focus on planning our journey. I've got a detailed map of the Sande Desert. Let's compare it with yours."

He retrieved his map, and together we spread them on the ground. I circled a spot on my map with a red pen and asked, "Is this where you were?"

Mateo nodded. "Yes."

"And the virtual image you saw, how far do you think it was?" I asked.

"About half a mile," he replied.

I marked another circle on the map. Two small circles now stood out—one marking Mateo's location, the other the estimated position of the mirage.

"Twenty miles from there is an oasis," I pointed out. "It's marked on the map—Yali Oasis. How about we start our search from there?"

"Okay, let's start from there," Mateo agreed, though his response seemed automatic, his spirit dulled by the weight of his quest.

I couldn't help but worry about what would happen if we never found the Arab girl. His current state was concerning enough.

"We can't venture into the desert without proper preparation," I said. "We'll need to stay here for at least three or four days to get ready."

Again, Mateo simply nodded, his enthusiasm dampened by fatigue and obsession.

Realizing that his current state was unsustainable, I assigned him tasks to occupy his mind and channel his energy. I asked him to handle purchasing supplies for our desert journey.

Meanwhile, I set out to find a vehicle robust enough to withstand the challenges of a long desert expedition.

As we each focused on our tasks, I hoped that the promise of action would lift Mateo's spirits and bring us closer to his elusive dream.

I spent the day tracking down an excellent vehicle for our journey. The car belonged to the chief of a small tribe near Shur Port. While his domain covered less than 100 square kilometers, he was among the wealthiest individuals in the region.

The car, custom-built in Germany, boasted every comfort imaginable. I secured it through an introduction from an Arab friend, and as I met the chief, I realized my efforts before arriving in Shur Port had not been in vain. In the chief's bedroom, I noticed a photo of the Arab girl—the very one I had distributed through various contacts.

However, my relief was short-lived. The chief, admiring the photo, remarked, "I can't believe such a beautiful girl exists in Arabia. I must find her and make her my wife!"

Driving the chief's luxurious car back to Shur Port, a sense of unease settled over me. While Flora's idea of distributing the girl's photo had seemed promising, it also presented unforeseen complications. The most powerful and affluent sheikhs in the Arab world were notorious for their desires. If Mateo had been captivated by the girl's image, so too might these influential men. Should the girl reside within a sheikh's domain, the situation could escalate into a grave tragedy.

Regret gnawed at me for choosing this approach. Yet, when I reunited with Mateo, I held my tongue about my concerns. He was already in a fragile state, and burdening him with additional worries might shatter his physical state entirely, rendering him unable to join me in the search for Sandy. In silence, I resolved to press forward, hoping our efforts would lead to a more fortunate outcome.

CHAPTER 3

THE MOST VICIOUS BANDIT IN THE DESERT

We embarked on our journey early the next morning under a vast, cloudless sky. An hour into the drive, our car had ventured deep into the desert. The sand stretched out before us, undulating like the waves of a vast sea. Yet unlike the lively ocean, these desert waves were still and lifeless, emanating a daunting sense of despair.

Before leaving, Mateo and I agreed to take turns driving. He insisted on taking the first leg, eager to revisit the spot where he last glimpsed Sandy's elusive mirage.

By noon, we arrived at the location. Mateo stepped out, his feet sinking into the sand. He pointed ahead. "It was right there. Last time, she was right in front—"

I followed his gaze, but saw only the endless expanse of desert. Mateo stood motionless, hoping for the mirage to reappear. Yet, the horizon offered nothing but the stark contrast of pale yellow sand and azure sky.

After a long silence, Mateo sighed and climbed back into the car, murmuring, "She refuses to appear again."

Annoyed, I asked, "Mateo, are you chasing a mirage, or searching for a real person?"

He gave a bitter smile. "Until I find the real person, seeing her mirage would be some comfort."

There was no point arguing with someone so captivated by his vision. I simply said, "In about an hour, we'll reach Yali Oasis."

Mateo resumed driving, and as our vehicle moved forward, it left deep ruts in the sand. But the desert, deceptive in its stillness, slowly consumed the tracks, erasing them within moments, as if swallowing us whole.

An hour later, scattered palm trees appeared on the horizon, like an isolated island amidst the sea of sand. We drove another half-mile and finally reached Yali Oasis.

The oasis was a miracle amid the harsh desert—a large, clear lake surrounded by lush greenery, with two smaller lakes nearby. Tents and simple structures dotted the landscape. Arabs led camels among the tents, creating a lively market atmosphere.

As we parked by the lake, the locals regarded us with respect, recognizing the chief's car. I stepped out and waved to an Arab.

The man hesitated before approaching. I began, "We're looking for someone—"

Before I could continue, Mateo interjected, "Don't waste time here. She isn't here."

I turned, puzzled. "How can you be sure?"

He gestured around us. "The environment in the photo—does it match this place?"

He was right; the setting in the photo was entirely different. Still, I clung to hope, showing the photo. "Has anyone seen this girl?"Privately, I hoped the tribal chiefs wouldn't find her. Their intentions were likely self-serving, and if they found Sandy, it wouldn't be for Mateo's benefit.

I turned away, avoiding Mateo's gaze, worried my face might betray my concern. "There's no sign of her in Yali Oasis. Where should we head next?"

"It's up to you," Mateo replied, his voice resigned. "I have no idea."

We switched seats, and I took the wheel, steering us slowly through the oasis.

As we passed, I noticed many Arab women, their faces veiled, balancing water jars or baskets on their heads. Their identities were hidden, shrouded in mystery.

A thought occurred to me, and as we drove out of the oasis, I voiced it. "Mateo, did you notice that in the photos you took, none of the Arab women were veiled?"

"Yes," he nodded, realization dawning.

"Isn't that unusual?" I pressed. "When do Arab women typically unveil their faces?"

He furrowed his brow, thinking. "In front of people they know well—"

He paused, a light of understanding sparking in his eyes. "I get it. Sandy must live in a small, close-knit oasis where the women don't need to cover their faces regularly."

"Exactly!" I exclaimed, sharing his excitement.

Yet, the excitement was short-lived. Mateo's expression soon turned somber, realizing our insight offered no concrete help in finding Sandy.

Since leaving Yali Oasis, I meticulously documented each stop. But after more than 40 days, each entry read the same: no discovery.

Four days ago, we ran out of fuel. We contacted the chief by radio, requesting a small plane to drop supplies. But no fuel came—either the chief couldn't locate us, or he had retracted his aid.

The desert stretched endlessly, a harsh reminder of our diminishing resources and hope. Yet, amidst the vast emptiness, our resolve remained, driven by the faint glimpse of a dream that refused to fade.

The blistering sun hung high in the sky, casting long shadows across the endless sea of sand. For two days, Mateo and I had watched the horizon, hoping for salvation. Finally, a caravan of camels appeared, their silhouettes a mirage against the blinding light. With no other choice, we abandoned our once-gleaming car to the desert's voracious appetite and joined the caravan's slow, rhythmic march.

The camels plodded along, their pace a stark contrast to the speed of our forsaken vehicle. For two interminable days, the barren desert stretched out in all directions, an unending ocean of sand meeting the sky. The dry wind was relentless, and our skin began to crack like parched earth. We wrapped ourselves in cloth, adopting the practices of the seasoned Arab travelers around us.

By day, the sun was a merciless fireball, baking us beneath its relentless glare. By night, the desert transformed under the moon's pale glow, a haunting landscape of silence and shadows. The Arabs seemed at ease in this alien world, but for Mateo and me, it was as if we had crash-landed on a distant, inhospitable planet.

Eight days we journeyed with the caravan until it reached its destination, only to join another. The routine became a blur, and any attempt at documenting our travels felt futile. We were no longer explorers; we were automatons, trudging onward without purpose.

Time lost all meaning in the desert's monotony. Days melded into one another, and sanity felt like a fragile thread. How many days had passed since we left the car? I had no answer. The only certainty was that we had changed camel teams five times, crossed five sprawling oases, and countless smaller ones, yet Sandy remained as elusive as the shifting dunes.

That night, we found refuge in an abandoned earthen city, its once-thriving life now reduced to dust and memories. The pool that had sustained it was a cracked basin, with only thick mud at its heart; the palm trees that once stood sentinel were long dead. As the sun dipped below the horizon, we entered a ghost town, greeted only by the watchful eyes of marmots.

The Arabs reveled in their find, grateful for shelter better than the sand beside the camels. Mateo and I settled within the crumbling walls, smoking spicy Arab tobacco in silence.

After a long pause, Mateo spoke, his voice a dry whisper. "You shouldn't do this kind of stupid thing anymore."

A bitter smile crept onto my lips. "If it's stupid, we shouldn't do it anymore."

He shook his head, stubbornness etched into his features. "I'm different. I've found Sandy. I have my reasons. But you? What do you gain?"

"I hope," I said slowly, "that by staying with you, you'll see the folly in this quest. Let's leave together."

Mateo fell silent, contemplating my words. In that moment, a flicker of hope ignited within me. If he agreed, we could escape this desolate maze and reclaim our lives.

Amidst the unforgiving desert, where abandoning him seemed the logical escape to comfort, I found myself tethered by a deeper force. Mateo's aimless wandering haunted my thoughts, preventing my departure. His gaze, however, met mine with an unyielding resolve.

"No, I won't leave. I'm going to look for more," he declared, his eyes hardened with determination.

In that instant, the flicker of hope within me was swallowed by the vast, unyielding darkness of the desert night.

Inwardly, I sighed, accepting his decision with a quiet resignation. He had turned down my offer, yet I masked my disappointment with a casual shrug. "Alright, then. I won't leave for now. I'll stay with you."

Mateo's voice was a low murmur. "You will leave sooner or later."

"True," I conceded. "I can't stay forever. But for now, I'm here."

We lay back on the straw mats we had salvaged from the ruins. Though frayed and weathered by time, they served as a modest cushion against the hard ground. Around us, the Arabs from the caravan shared laughter, their voices a comforting cadence in the cool desert night. Above, the sky was a tapestry of stars, more brilliant and numerous than I'd ever seen. I wondered if this celestial display was unique to the desert or if it was just the clarity of my own perception, sharpened by the vast emptiness surrounding us.

Slowly, sleep claimed us, not out of peace, but necessity. We needed rest to endure the next day's grueling journey across the camel's swaying backs.

I awoke abruptly to a cacophony of shouts and clattering noise. Jolted upright, I found Mateo already alert, his eyes wide with confusion. Torches flared in the darkness, their light casting long, dancing shadows. Before we could comprehend the chaos, four men, clad in flowing white robes, leaped over the earthen walls. They brandished gleaming Arab scimitars, the moonlight catching their blades with an ominous glint.

One of them barked an order in a harsh dialect, demanding we rise. Mateo hesitated, bewildered. "Get up," I urged him in a hurried whisper. "Don't resist. These are the most ruthless robbers of the desert."

Mateo's face blanched as we stood. The robbers seized us, dragging us out into the open.

In the clearing, a grim scene unfolded. Scores of robbers, twenty or thirty strong, all clad in white, surrounded the subdued caravan. Three bodies lay motionless on the sand, silent witnesses to the brutality of our captors. They had either fallen in a futile resistance or been slain as a warning to the rest.

Herded together, we watched helplessly as the robbers looted the camels, stripping them of goods and precious water. Desperation simmered among us, and one Arab, driven by thirst, broke ranks to plead for mercy. "Leave us some water!" he cried out.

His voice was a lone spark in the night, quickly extinguished. Two scimitars flashed, and he crumpled, his plea silenced forever in a pool of crimson.

The scene unfolded in a blur of adrenaline and instinct. Seeing the fallen Arab, something primal surged within me. I shouted and charged forward, my foot kicking up sand as I struck one of the robbers squarely in the face. He reeled back, clutching his face, and in that brief window of opportunity, I seized his scimitar.

With the blade now in my grasp, I pivoted to meet another assailant. Our swords clashed in a rapid dance of steel, the desert air ringing with each parry and thrust. Though skilled, these desert marauders had not met someone like me, honed by countless hours of practice and driven by desperation.

In three swift blows, I found my opening. I spun, the sharp edge of my scimitar slicing through the air. It grazed past the robber's side, and he staggered backward, collapsing as crimson seeped through his white robes.

Time seemed to suspend in the immediate aftermath, a heavy silence settling over the scene. It was a fleeting calm, shattered seconds later by a chorus of shouts as the bandits rallied. They abandoned their loot, encircling me with fervor in their eyes.

Mateo's voice pierced the clamor, a beacon of concern. "Don't be afraid," I called back, my voice steady. "I can handle them!"

The bandits closed in, their fallen comrade forgotten in their eagerness to confront me. Their shouts were an unintelligible cacophony, yet I stood my ground, scimitar poised.

Suddenly, their cries ceased, parting to reveal a towering figure stepping forward. His presence commanded respect, and the scimitar he wielded was a formidable weapon—larger and more menacing than any I'd seen.

With a swift motion, he swung his blade in a wide arc, the air whistling as the steel cut through it. The circle of light lingered, a dazzling testament to his skill.

His intent was clear. This was no mere thug, but a warrior, acknowledging my prowess and inviting a duel. I had unwittingly earned their respect; they didn't seek to overwhelm me with numbers but to test my mettle in single combat.

The realization struck me then. My defense against their comrades had not incited their wrath but rather their admiration, challenging me to prove myself against their champion.

The tall Arab bandit, clearly the leader of this desert horde, loomed before me, a formidable opponent. Instinctively, I knew that defeating him would earn the respect of the entire band, though the cost might be my very life. Yet, in this moment, there was no room for hesitation or retreat — only the certainty of the fight.

Matching his challenge, I swung my scimitar in a wide arc, signaling my acceptance. The leader nodded, his eyes narrowing with focus, and the surrounding bandits erupted into cheers, the night air electrified with anticipation.

With a powerful leap, the bandit lunged at me, his scimitar slicing through the air with deadly intent. I raised my blade, meeting his strike with a resounding clang that reverberated up my arms, forcing me back a step. The strength behind his blow was staggering, and as his blade descended again, it narrowly missed my face, leaving a chill in its wake.

I countered swiftly, aiming for his wrist, but he deftly evaded, launching another strike. Realizing the futility of matching his brute force, I evaded his attack with a roll, anticipating his pursuit. As he advanced, I seized the chance, swinging my scimitar low to catch his legs while rolling to safety.

In the chaos of movement, I couldn't be certain if my blade had found its mark. But then a guttural roar confirmed it. Rising to my feet, I saw blood seeping from the leader's left leg—a testament to my strike.

In a gesture of honor, I pinched the tip of my scimitar with my left hand, signaling my advantage and my desire to end the duel. It was a traditional sign of respect, indicating I had gained the upper hand and was willing to stop the fight.

In my naivety, I had forgotten that these were not honorable warriors but ruthless bandits, thirsty for blood. The leader's primal roar shattered the silence, and suddenly, the bandits surged toward me like a relentless tide.

I barely had time to react before my arms were seized from behind, rendering my scimitar useless. The ambush was swift and brutal; I had misjudged their intent entirely. The world spun as I struggled, my feet lashing out instinctively, connecting with the faces of two assailants. But it was a futile resistance.

A sharp blow landed on the back of my head, and the world turned upside down. Nausea clawed at my stomach as darkness swallowed me whole.

When I awoke, a searing pain branded my skull, yanking me from unconsciousness. I blinked against the darkness, disoriented, and realized a leather bag covered my head. In the shrouded blackness, I felt the steady rhythm of the camel beneath me, each step reverberating through my bound body. The cool night air whispered past my skin, confirming the cover of darkness that still cloaked the desert.

As the memories of the ambush flooded back, the reality of my capture settled in with a grim clarity. I was in the hands of the robbers, trussed up like a prize to be paraded. The pain in my head was a constant reminder of the brutality I had faced, but I bit back any groans, forcing myself to remain silent and composed.

Bound hand and foot, I wondered where these bandits were taking me and what fate awaited me. My journey with Mateo, initially a quest to find the mysterious Arab girl he claimed to have seen in a mirage, had led to this perilous situation. Thoughts of Mateo filled my mind—was he captured too, or worse, had he fallen to the robbers' blades?

With no power to change my circumstances, I resolved to wait, to bide my time until I could discern their intentions or find an opportunity to escape. The camel beneath me continued its relentless pace, each jolt sending a wave of discomfort through my body. My stomach pressed awkwardly against its back, the ride a relentless torment.

After what seemed like an endless journey, the camel finally came to a stop. I heard a cacophony of voices, a chorus of cheers interwoven with inquisitive calls, mostly from women. "Are you back? What did you catch this time?" Their words were casual, almost routine, as if my capture was just another day's work for them.

A bitter smile tugged at my lips. Realization dawned on me like a harsh desert sun—I was in the clutches of not just a group of bandits, but an entire tribe. The desert had its own hierarchy, and among the Arab ethnic groups, some were peaceful, others fierce, but none more formidable than this nomadic tribe of marauders, masters of the shifting sands.

In the harsh conditions of the desert, survival had winnowed out the weak, leaving behind only the most ruthless and skilled. These were a people forged in adversity, adept with the scimitar and relentless in their pursuits. During World War II, such tribes had been pivotal in desert warfare, and their descendants still roamed the Sahara, their numbers diminished but their ferocity undimmed.

I had never imagined encountering such a tribe in the Sande Desert. Yet here I was, a captive among them, where even women and children viewed banditry as a way of life. I struggled against my bindings, but they held fast, a testament to their captors' experience.

The camel beneath me slowed its pace, signaling our arrival at their encampment. The relentless jostling eased, but my predicament remained dire. With no means of escape, I could only resign myself to whatever fate awaited.

The cacophony of voices around me quieted, replaced by the astonishing sound of gurgling water. In the heart of the desert, such a sound was miraculous, almost a mirage of its own. Yet it was real, and I strained to catch my bearings.

A man spoke in a rough, unfamiliar tongue, the words lost on me. This tribe, isolated and insular, had preserved their language, a secret only they shared. As he spoke, I felt a hand patting my back repeatedly, the man who had dueled with me, introducing me to unseen eyes.

Suddenly, I was shoved from the camel, tumbling through the air. The ground rushed up to meet me, and in that brief descent, I braced for impact, hoping against hope that I would not suffer injury. In this hostile land, a broken bone could spell the end.

To my astonishment, I landed on a soft felt carpet, sparing me from injury. I lay still, listening to a murmur of voices that soon faded into silence. The leather bag was then pulled from my head, and I winced against the sudden flood of light. Blinking, I took in my surroundings.

I found myself inside a cavernous structure, possibly built into a natural cave, with steep rock walls framing the space. A rich scarlet carpet lay beneath me, and a massive red curtain swayed gently before me. It was clear that many eyes were watching from behind its folds.

Two imposing Arab warriors stood nearby, their expressions unreadable. Torches flickered in the rock crevices, casting dancing shadows across the walls. My hands and feet remained bound, and I had no clue what fate awaited me.

Then, from behind a yellow curtain, an Arab man emerged. He approached with a smile and spoke in unexpectedly fluent English. "Sorry to have put you through this." he said, his tone disarming.

My surprise rendered me speechless. He continued, "Is it strange? I am a doctor of law from the university!"

I stared, bewildered, as he gestured to the warriors. With a swift, practiced motion, they drew their scimitars. My heart seized as the blades flashed toward me. In that instant, terror gripped me—the fear of imminent death.

But instead of striking me down, the blades sliced through the ropes binding my wrists and ankles. The warriors stepped back, their movements precise and controlled, leaving me unscathed.

I marveled at their skill, still processing the unexpected turn of events. The man smiled again, a hint of amusement in his eyes. "Please stand up."

I pressed my hands to the earth, feeling the grit beneath my palms as I rose. The bindings had been too tight, too long, and my limbs protested with a tingling numbness that threatened to topple me. But pride anchored me—I refused to collapse before them. I rubbed my wrists, coaxing life back into them, while steadying myself.

"My name is Pengdu," the Arab said, extending a hand—a gesture of unexpected camaraderie.

I clasped his hand, offering my own name in return, though my mind was elsewhere, racing with questions and concerns.

Pengdu's gaze sharpened, disbelief flickering across his features. "They say you fought Sidula and bested him?"

Sidula—the name resonated, a shadowy figure in the chaos of the earthen city. I shrugged, feigning nonchalance. "That was nothing."

Pengdu laughed, a sound rich with admiration and surprise. "Nothing? Sidula is our tribe's second warrior, a master of the sword!"

I had little interest in tribal rankings or swordsmanship. My thoughts were tethered to more pressing matters. "What about my companion? How is he?"

Pengdu's eyebrows lifted, curiosity piqued. "Your companion?"

"Yes," I pressed, urgency creeping into my voice, "in the camel caravan you intercepted, there was another man with me, Mr. Mateo."

Pengdu's laughter erupted, echoing in the vastness around us. "Then that Mr. Mateo must be a coward!"

The puzzle deepened, layers of mystery unfolding before me, as I stood in the heart of the unknown, where every answer only birthed more questions.

CHAPTER 4

DUEL WITH THE DESERT'S MASTER BLADESMAN

The words hung in the air, enigmatic and charged. "What do you mean?" I asked, my mind racing to catch up.

Pengdu's smile was a blend of amusement and intrigue. "When Sidula and his men knocked you out, bound you, and took you away, not a soul rose in your defense. It seems your friend was nowhere to be found. He must have been hiding, too scared to act."

Relief washed over me. At least Mateo was safe. He was still in the earthen city with the Arabs, part of the camel caravan. They would eventually leave, and Mateo would continue to shadow them, unharmed.

I couldn't fault Mateo for not intervening during my capture—he was no swordsman, unfamiliar with wielding an Arab scimitar. Even if he had stood up, what difference could it have made?

"Why did you bring me here?" I asked, curiosity and caution intertwining in my voice.

My gaze drifted behind the curtain, an inexplicable sense of being watched gnawing at me. Though I saw no one, the feeling was undeniable.

"Don't worry," Pengdu reassured, his voice smooth and calming.

He clapped his hands, a sharp "pa pa" echoing in the room. In response, four robust Arabs entered. Two carried a low table, another a rich red felt, and the fourth a large platter of exquisite dishes.

Since venturing into the Arabian Desert, such a feast was a rarity. My stomach growled in anticipation as the table was set before me. With a nod, Pengdu invited me, "Please, sit."

I settled cross-legged on the red felt, the enticing aroma of the food enveloping me.

"Don't be shy," Pengdu urged. "We may not have much, but the wine is exceptional."

I lifted a hefty glass, savoring a sip. The honey-roasted lamb was succulent, a delight I devoured with abandon. In that moment, whatever fate awaited me seemed distant, eclipsed by the joy of a good meal.

For half an hour, I ate heartily, finally leaning back with a satisfied sigh.

Pengdu observed me throughout, his expression unreadable but kind. As I finished, he spoke again, "I mentioned Sidula was our tribe's second-best warrior, and you defeated him."

I nodded, wiping my lips. "If he doubts it, I'm ready to face him again."

"No need," Pengdu replied. "He accepts his defeat. However, our tribe's number one knifeman, our revered leader, seeks to challenge you."

I was momentarily taken aback. "Alright, I'll be ready to face him. When? Now?"

Pengdu shook his head with a smile of understanding. "Not yet. You need to rest first. We believe in fairness—a true warrior emerges from a fair competition," he said with a tone of reverence.

I nodded, acknowledging his respect for the warrior's code. "Where should I rest?"

"Follow me," Pengdu instructed, leading the way.

We approached a red curtain, and upon parting it, a narrow passage lay before us—clearly a natural cave. Ten steps in, Pengdu unveiled another red curtain.

Behind it lay a small cave, transformed into a cozy room with a large, inviting bed. "Rest here," Pengdu offered.

With a subtle clap of his hands, two Arab women entered, their faces partially veiled. "They'll tend to your needs," Pengdu said, smiling.

I raised my hand in polite refusal. "Thank you, but I prefer solitude. If I'm to duel with your tribe's finest, a genuine rest is what I need."

Pengdu chuckled, dismissing the women with a wave. He exited, leaving me alone.

Exhausted, I sank into the bed, my body grateful for the reprieve. As I lay there, my mind wandered, replaying the encounter with Sidula. His defeat had come with surprising ease, yet I couldn't shake the looming challenge ahead.

The tribe's number one knifeman was a different story. His prowess undoubtedly surpassed Sidula's. How much better, though? Could I best him, too? Victory would surely bring respect and favor, but failure could spell disaster—perhaps even a bloody end.

These thoughts circled briefly before sleep enveloped me, deep and restorative.

When I awoke, the soft glow of torches still illuminated the room. My body felt renewed, suggesting I had slept for over ten hours.

I leaped from the bed, stretching, and was met by an Arab woman carrying water. Another followed, bearing a large pot of camel milk.

After washing and drinking deeply, Pengdu arrived, his presence warm and welcoming. "What time is it?" I asked.

"It's the afternoon of the second day," he replied with a grin. "Think it's time for a bath?"

A joyous laugh escaped me. "Perfect!"

"Follow me," Pengdu beckoned, leading me toward the promise of refreshing waters.

As I followed Pengdu through the narrow passage and into the sprawling lobby, I could feel the weight of curious eyes upon me, each gaze tinged with intrigue and suspicion. It was as if they knew something I did not, a secret whispered through the desert sands that I was yet to uncover.

Emerging from the cavernous depths of the great cave, I was greeted by a sight both daunting and mesmerizing. Two towering cliffs rose from the desert floor like ancient sentinels, their rugged faces carved by time and wind. The first cliff served as a formidable natural barrier, concealing a hidden oasis that lay nestled behind it. The second cliff, even more mysterious, housed the tribe's enigmatic residence.

Pengdu led me around this second monolith, revealing a small oasis that seemed to pulse with life. A tranquil pool reflected the azure sky, fringed by a cluster of palm trees swaying gently in the breeze. Nearby, women went about their tasks, washing clothes with a rhythm as timeless as the desert itself.

And then, it hit me—a scene so familiar it left me breathless, my heart pounding with recognition. This was the very place Mateo had glimpsed in his vision! An illusion, yes, but strikingly real in its vividness.

I halted, unable to mask the shock etched upon my face. Pengdu turned, his eyes questioning. "What's wrong with you?" he asked, his voice a tether to reality.

Words eluded me, and I could only point mutely at the pool. The women had moved on, yet the pool remained, a testament to Mateo's vision. There was no mistaking it.

Pengdu followed my gaze, his expression unperturbed, as if he had witnessed such revelations countless times before. "Did you see something unusual?" he pressed, his curiosity piqued by my astonishment.

I struggled to find my voice, finally managing, "No—it's just that this scene reminded me of a dream."

Pengdu chuckled knowingly. "Not a dream, perhaps. More likely, you saw this place in a mirage while wandering the desert. It's not uncommon."

His insight struck me with the force of a revelation. How could he know? Yet, it was true. I nodded slowly, the pieces of a larger puzzle clicking into place.

The mirage Mateo had spoken of was no mere illusion—it was this very oasis. The realization was electrifying. I had stumbled upon the place I'd long sought, and somewhere here, hidden among the palm trees and whispers of wind, was the Arab girl with the gentle, captivating smile. The girl entwined with the thieves, a paradox of beauty and intrigue.

But the question loomed large—how could I find her in this labyrinth of secrets and shadows?

I turned to Pengdu, confessing, "Indeed, I've seen this pool and those trees in the mirage."

Pengdu's smile was enigmatic, "It seems the mirage has left quite an impression on you!"

I merely smiled, choosing silence over revelation. In the intricate chess game unfolding before us, Pengdu was no ally. He stood as an adversary, a shadowed figure in the looming tapestry of conflict. Soon, I would face their tribe's foremost swordsman in a duel of scimitars, a dance of death where only one would emerge victorious. The stakes were clear, and the path fraught with peril, yet the fire of determination burned within me. This was a battle not just of blades, but of wits and survival.

As we neared the pool, I cast a casual question his way, "How large is your tribe? Would my taking a bath here pollute your water source?"

He chuckled, a sound as rough as the desert wind. "Fear not, the true God watches over us. An underground river feeds this oasis, sustaining over 700 of our people amidst the endless sands."

The revelation hit me with the force of a desert storm — over 700 souls reside within this hidden enclave. Assuming an even split between men and women, my quest to find the Arab girl would mean sifting through a sea of over 300 faces. Under different circumstances, with time as my ally, the task might have been manageable. But tonight, destiny hangs in the balance. The impending duel casts a long shadow over my efforts, leaving me vulnerable and pressed for time. In the face of such uncertainty, the search for the Arab girl becomes a daunting challenge. The sands of time slip through my fingers, each grain a reminder of the urgency fueling my every step.

We reached the pool's edge, and I paused, turning to Pengdu. "Pardon my modesty, but I'm not accustomed to bathing with an audience."

With a knowing nod, he relented, "Very well. You know the way. Once you're done, join me in the big cave."

I watched him retreat, his figure soon swallowed by the desert's embrace. Alone, I turned to the pool, finding towels and fresh clothes awaiting me. Shedding the dust and tension of the journey, I plunged into the cool waters, the relief palpable as the desert's grasp loosened its hold.

Emerging refreshed, I dressed in the new garments, the absence of onlookers a welcome reprieve. An opportunity presented itself, one too tempting to ignore. Why rush to the cave when the village lay open before me, a tapestry of secrets waiting to be unraveled?

Venturing forward, I skirted the cliff, my heart a compass guiding me deeper into the tribe's sanctuary. Stone houses clustered like ancient whispers, a testament to resilience. Another pool, larger and bustling with life, came into view. Women, their faces unveiled, went about their tasks, their presence adding vibrancy to the austere landscape.

Among them, she could be waiting—the Arab girl, the key to unraveling the mystery that had drawn me here. As I moved among them, I knew the path ahead was fraught with danger and discovery, but the promise of answers propelled me forward, each step echoing with the rhythm of fate.

As I approached the large pool, the air seemed to shift, charged with an energy that was both curious and cautious. Dozens of women turned their gaze upon me, their eyes filled with a strange curiosity that belied the traditional reserve of Arab women who typically avert their eyes and retreat in the presence of men. I met their stares with my own, searching for a familiar face among them.

To my astonishment, many were strikingly beautiful, yet the one I sought—the Arab girl—was absent from their ranks. A pang of disappointment tugged at me, compounded by the loss of her photograph. Had I possessed it, the task of inquiring about her would have been far simpler, yielding answers with minimal effort. My attempts to engage them in conversation were met with polite, enigmatic smiles, offering no clues to the mystery I longed to unravel.

Lingering by the pool, my thoughts raced as I pondered my next move. The tranquil moment was abruptly shattered by Pengdu's hurried approach, flanked by several men. His voice, laced with reprimand, cut through the air, "Why are you wandering around? Didn't I instruct you to return to me immediately?"

Frustration ignited within me, and my voice rose in defiance. "What does this imply? Am I a prisoner here? If so, you should have made that clear from the start!"

My indignation seemed to quell his irritation, and he responded with a composed urgency, "That's not my intention. The knife-fighting ceremony is about to commence."

Acknowledging his words with a terse nod, I followed him back to the cave, my thoughts a storm of anticipation and unease.

Upon entering the cave, the reason for the absence of men outside became clear. They had gathered here, a solemn assembly seated in two rows against the cave walls, forming a silent, watchful circle. Their expressions were grave, the atmosphere charged with an unspoken tension. The only sound was the soft crackle of torches, their flames dancing shadows across the stone.

Pengdu guided me to the center of this circle, motioning for me to remain still before stepping back into the shadows.

Two men approached, hefting a large box with deliberate care, and squatted before me.

As I carefully lifted the lid of the ornate box, the gleam of eight Arab scimitars met my gaze. Each blade was unique in its design, some with a pronounced curve, others barely bent at the tip; their lengths varied from long and sweeping to short and precise. They lay nestled against a bright red velvet pad, an exquisite setting for instruments of death. The juxtaposition was striking — a murder weapon presented with such reverence and care.

Pengdu stood beside me, his voice calm and instructive. "Choose the knife that suits you best," he commanded.

Conscious of my limitations with these exotic weapons, I carefully selected a scimitar with a relatively straight blade. A highly curved scimitar demanded skills I had not yet mastered. This particular blade, however, felt more familiar in my grip—an extension of my determination and resolve.

As soon as I claimed my weapon, the two men holding the box withdrew, their task complete.

Testing the edge of the blade with a gentle scrape, I confirmed its lethal sharpness. It was a weapon capable of slicing through the air with precision, severing a silk scarf in mid-flight.

With the knife in hand, Pengdu also retreated, leaving me alone in the center of the cave. A heavy silence descended, broken only by the rhythmic crackle of the torches, their light dancing along the blade's polished surface.

I stood poised, breath held, awaiting the emergence of my opponent—the tribe's preeminent swordsman. My fate rested on this duel, a pivotal moment that demanded every ounce of my skill and courage.

Time stretched, a mere minute feeling like an eternity, until Pengdu's sudden shout pierced the silence, a signal that sent a ripple of anticipation through the gathered assembly. Instinctively, I lowered my stance, prepared for a sudden assault.

Yet, the threat did not materialize as expected. Instead, two towering Arabs, over six feet five inches tall, emerged from behind a massive yellow curtain. Their sheer size was imposing, but I recognized that their bulk could hinder their agility, a crucial disadvantage in the art of swordplay. These men were not my adversaries.

Without sparing me a glance, they moved to draw back the curtain, revealing what lay beyond.

And there, framed by the flickering torchlight, stood my true opponent.

My opponent emerged from behind the curtain, a stark contrast to the towering figures who had preceded him. He was notably shorter, standing five or six inches beneath my own height, yet his presence was anything but diminutive. In his hand, he gripped a uniquely curved, half-moon-shaped scimitar, a weapon that seemed an extension of his very being.

Draped in a voluminous white robe that enveloped him like a shroud, his appearance was both enigmatic and imposing. A white cloth wrapped around his head obscured all but his eyes and hands, lending him an air of mystery.

As he advanced a few steps, I observed the fluid grace in his movements—a hallmark of a seasoned knifeman. His steps were feather-light, betraying a mastery of balance and control. His hands, almost elegant in their softness, reminded me of a pianist's—capable of coaxing both beauty and lethality from the blade they wielded.

He stopped mere feet from me, and the air between us crackled with tension. I drew a deep breath, steadying myself for what was to come. Pengdu stepped between us then, a mediator of the impending duel.

He reached out, grasping the tips of our scimitars, drawing them together until they intersected — a ceremonial gesture binding us to the duel's sacred code. His voice was firm and resolute, echoing through the cave, "Once I step back and raise my hand, you may begin. Anyone who attacks prematurely will face the wrath of the true God."

As Pengdu retreated, each step was a countdown to the inevitable clash, my heart pounding in sync with the rhythm of the moment. My initial focus had been on him, intent on catching the precise moment when his hand would signal the start. Yet, the intensity of my opponent's gaze drew me back to the present. His eyes, steady and penetrating, served as a stark reminder that even a moment's inattention could prove costly — a lesson I absorbed just in time.

Startled by this realization, I shifted my focus squarely onto my adversary. Pengdu continued his measured retreat, and with a sudden shout, he raised his hand high, signaling the beginning of the duel. The torchlight flickered, casting our shadows into sharp relief against the cave walls, and in that instant, it felt as though the world itself held its breath, suspended in the tension of the moment.

Startled by the realization, I shifted my focus squarely onto my adversary. Pengdu continued his measured withdrawal, and with a sudden shout, he raised his hand high, signaling the start. The torchlight flickered, casting our shadows into sharp relief, and in that instant, the world seemed to hold its breath.

Our blades, once touching, parted with a swift, practiced grace. In unison, we each stepped back, neither willing to rush into the fray. In that brief pause, my respect for my opponent deepened. He was not one to squander energy on hasty strikes; he was a strategist, waiting for the perfect moment to unleash a decisive blow. A true master would fight with such patience and precision.

My body instinctively adopted a slight crouch, mirroring the posture of my opponent. We maintained eye contact, a silent communication passing between us as we slowly pivoted, each completing a half-circle—a cautious dance of repositioning that kept us in constant anticipation of the other's move.

The silence in the cave was profound, amplifying the tension that hung thick in the air. No one dared to disrupt the quiet, as if even the slightest sound might shatter the fragile equilibrium.

As we completed our turn, I noted that my opponent showed no immediate intention of drawing his blade. This lack of aggression prompted me to test the waters.

With deliberate caution, I extended my scimitar forward, a calculated feint designed to gauge his response. The blade barely left its resting position before I retracted it, but in that brief moment, my opponent's blade flashed into action.

The air rang with a sharp "clang" as our blades met, the sound reverberating through the silent cave.

Though I had retracted my blade swiftly, my opponent's deft maneuver had already caught the tip, twisting his wrist with precision to send my weapon swinging outward.

In that split second, his scimitar sliced towards my chest with unerring accuracy. Instinctively, I stepped back, but the momentum was already against me. His relentless assault was like a tidal wave, forcing me to dodge and weave, each movement a desperate bid to regain control. Yet, despite my efforts, I found no opening to seize the upper hand. Within minutes, sweat poured down my face, my body taxed by the exertion.

His blade danced around me, a whirlwind of steel—up, down, left, right—a seamless extension of his will. The unique curvature of his scimitar seemed to bend the very air, encircling me with its perilous arc. It was as if the weapon itself was alive, guided by a master hand.

I marshaled every ounce of strength and cunning to dodge his attacks. Each narrowly avoided strike reverberated like thunder in the confined space. My breath came in ragged gasps, sweat stinging my eyes, blurring my vision. The oppressive heat and the relentless pace of the duel pushed me inexorably toward the brink, teetering on the precipice of defeat.

Then, a fleeting opportunity presented itself. In that critical moment, I finally saw an opening. The opponent's scimitar arced toward my face, and with a swift motion, I raised my blade, successfully intercepting it with a resounding "clang." This marked only the second time I had managed to deflect his unpredictable strikes, and for an instant, hope flickered within me. Perhaps, I thought, this was the turning point—a chance to reverse my fortune.

But I was sorely mistaken.

Barely had the sound of clashing steel faded when his scimitar, with a fluid grace that belied its lethal intent, descended toward my left leg. My reaction was swift, stepping aside with all the speed I could muster. Yet, despite my efforts, I was a heartbeat too slow. A chilling sensation swept over my leg, followed by a sharp, searing pain that drove the breath from my lungs.

Instinctively, I retreated, leaping back to gain distance. As I did, a heavy drop of blood splattered onto the cave floor, stark against the dusty ground. My opponent maintained his stance, his scimitar poised and ready, yet he did not press the advantage.

In that moment of stillness, the truth settled over me like a shroud—I had lost.

In that charged moment, a wave of shame and humiliation surged through me, igniting my blood with a fierce resolve. I glanced down, noting the wound on my left leg, a three-inch gash oozing a steady stream of blood. As if sensing the change within me, Pengdu approached.

The cheers in the cave hushed, leaving an expectant silence as he addressed me with slow, deliberate clarity, "You have already lost. You should throw down the knife in your hand and bow to our number one knifeman."

My face contorted with defiance, and my voice emerged unrecognizably hoarse, a single word escaping my lips: "No!" With a swift, decisive motion, I swung the knife, slicing off a strip of cloth to staunch my wound. As I bound the makeshift bandage to my leg, I raised my head defiantly and declared in Arabic, "I was just injured, not defeated!"

The reaction was immediate and electric. Every Arab in the cave rose to their feet, a wave of movement and rustling fabric filling the air, yet no words were spoken. Their eyes were fixed on me, the outsider who dared challenge their champion's victory.

Pengdu took a deep breath, his expression turning grave. "Do you know what this means?" he asked, his voice laden with gravity.

My reply was calm, unwavering. "Of course I know."

"You are proposing a duel to the death," Pengdu continued, his tone questioning if I truly grasped the enormity of my challenge. "Have you fully considered this?"

"I have," I replied coldly, cutting through his words. "Now, stop talking and step back."

Pengdu complied, retreating without further comment. The atmosphere in the cave was taut, charged with the anticipation of what was to come. All around, the Arabs took an involuntary step forward, their collective presence a testament to the gravity of the moment.

I had no time to decipher their expressions, no time to wonder if they saw me as courageous or foolish. Their opinions were irrelevant in the face of the task before me.

I had to focus on survival, on forging victory with the blade in my hand. Failure was not an option.

As I raised my knife, my opponent's eyes caught mine, gleaming with an intensity that mirrored my own. In that instant, our understanding was mutual. This was a duel of equals, and only one would emerge victorious.

I launched forward, my knife a blur as I thrust towards him. He retreated, and I pursued, each attack met with deft evasions. His scimitar moved with deadly elegance, and we danced a lethal ballet of attack and counterattack. My knife was once again deflected, but this time I was ready, adapting quickly and pressing the advantage. Unlike our last encounter, this duel was evenly matched, each of us testing the other's limits.

The ensuing ten minutes were a blur of motion and instinct, my mind lost in the rhythm of combat. Thoughts ceased, replaced by pure reaction and determination. But the wound on my leg continued to bleed, each step a reminder of my vulnerability, and my footing grew uncertain.

Then, suddenly, pain exploded across my shoulder as his scimitar grazed me—a mere touch, but enough to slice through flesh with ease. The sharp agony was immediate, causing my upper body to recoil instinctively, the wound a fresh reminder of the stakes.

I staggered momentarily, struggling to regain my balance as the throbbing in my shoulder joined the persistent ache in my leg.

In that critical moment, as my opponent's scimitar sliced the air above my head, I felt the brush of wind and saw strands of my hair cascading down. But the chaos of battle presented a fleeting opportunity—one I seized with all my might. As we closed the distance, I drove my left elbow into my opponent's waist with force and followed with a swift kick to the lower abdomen. The impact sent her sprawling backward.

My scimitar followed, slicing through the air, and in one swift motion, it caught the edge of the white cloth covering his face. The fabric tore away, revealing a face I never expected to see. She screamed, the sound piercing the air—a voice unmistakably feminine. It was the first sound she'd made since stepping from the curtain, and it was a cry that rocked my world.

The revelation struck me like a thunderbolt. My knife halted mid-swing, suspended in disbelief. The light from the blade illuminated her face, and I recognized her—Sandy. Though that was not her real name, it's what Mateo called her. She was the Arab girl I had been searching for all along.

Her eyes, cold and steely, met mine, and I saw beyond the warrior to the woman I had sought with such desperation. In that instant, all the anger and resolve drained away, leaving only recognition and shock.

I withdrew my blade, my voice erupting in an unintelligible shout, a primal expression of the myriad emotions and words I couldn't articulate. But as my cry echoed through the cave, she lunged, her scimitar plunging into my stomach.

Staggering back, I felt a dizzying wave of pain and shock. She fell, and the tumult of the cave closed in. The Arabs surged forward, their shouts melding into a cacophony as my world began to blur. I remained upright, but my body was betraying me. Sounds dissolved into a muffled haze, and as I bent forward, the darkness overtook me and I collapsed.

Time lost meaning, a blur of pain and oblivion.

When consciousness clawed its way back, it was thirst that roused me. My mouth felt as though it was being seared by fire, and the desperation for water was the first sensation that pierced the fog.

I opened my eyes to a world of blurred shapes and muted colors. Closing them again, I heard Pengdu's familiar voice, tinged with a mix of relief and urgency, "God, I just saw him open his eyes!"

Other voices murmured in the background, one distinctly Scottish, advising, "Don't make noise, he needs quiet!"

With effort, I reopened my eyes, greeted by the sight of a white man with a mustache peering down at me. His presence was unfamiliar, adding to my confusion.

Noticing my eyes flutter open, he leaned in urgently. "I'm a doctor. They brought me here to treat you. For God's sake, you need to recover—quickly!"

My voice barely a whisper, I asked, "What... what happened?"

His response was both calm and encouraging. "Considering the circumstances, you're doing well. Your injuries were severe, but with luck, you'll be back on your feet in a month."

"A month!" I echoed, the weight of time pressing down on me.

"You've already been here a month," the doctor added. "Another won't make much difference."

The revelation left me silent, grappling with the idea of being bedridden for so long. I couldn't fathom the passage of time—thirty days spent in a haze of unconsciousness.

I closed my eyes, wrestling with the question that loomed large in my mind: why was I still alive? The very act of pondering confirmed my existence, yet doubt lingered—was I still the same person I had been?

Driven by an insistent need for self-reassurance, I opened my eyes again and said with effort, "I want to see myself!"

The doctor, initially surprised by my request, asked, "What do you mean? Why do you want to see yourself?"

Straining against my weakened state, I repeated, "Let me see myself — I need to confirm my own existence!"

The doctor, understanding the urgency in my voice, straightened up and instructed, "Give him a mirror!"

Pengdu responded swiftly, relaying the request to another Arab, who left and returned shortly with a mirror. I tried to raise my hand to take it, but my strength failed me, my hand dropping back to the bed.

Gently, the doctor held the mirror before my eyes. "Where am I?" I cried out as I looked into it.

The reflection was both shocking and familiar—a visage I barely recognized. The face staring back was gaunt, skeletal, hair matted in disarray and a beard that had grown wild and unkempt. This was not the image of myself that I knew, yet undeniably, it was me.

The sight elicited a cry from my lips, a visceral reaction to the transformation. Overwhelmed, I closed my eyes once more. It became clear that a month of severe injury and unconsciousness had taken its toll, and expecting otherwise was unrealistic.

As I closed my eyes, Pengdu's words reached me, tinged with a mix of relief and warning. "Doctor, you are lucky. Look, he has woken up. If he died, you would have to die with him. Now, do your best to heal him!"

The doctor gave a rueful smile at Pengdu's remark. I took a few breaths, trying to gather my thoughts, and weakly called out, "Doctor, where are you from?"

I felt his reassuring hand on my shoulder. "Don't worry," he said softly, "I am part of your rescue."

His words left me momentarily stunned, their meaning unclear.

He continued, "After you were captured, one of your friends immediately alerted the local authorities, as well as your friends and family. They all rushed to the Sande Desert, but they couldn't find you."

He paused, then added, "I managed to bring a radio transmitter into the desert, but I was captured and brought here. Now, I want to give you an injection and send some good news to your family!"

The mention of my family caught me off guard. "My family—" I murmured, "You mean, my wife is here too?"

"Yes," he confirmed, "there are quite a few people, including the chiefs of four tribes. They're all gathered at Yali Oasis."

"Take me away from here," I pleaded with what little strength I had left. "Take me—to Yali Oasis!"

The doctor gave a weary smile. "No, first, your health condition is absolutely not suitable for any movement, and second, the leader here has ordered that you are not allowed to leave."

The leader here! The realization hit me like a wave. The leader was the number one knifeman of this tribe, the same enigmatic woman I had been searching for with Mateo.

The world spun, dizziness overtaking me. The doctor administered an injection, and mercifully, I slipped back into unconsciousness, the weight of the revelations swirling in the depths of my mind.

CHAPTER 5

BANDIT LEADER'S WEDDING

When I regained consciousness again, the scene around me had changed slightly. There were now two doctors by my side, tending to my needs. The original doctor nodded towards the newcomer, explaining, "He just arrived from Yali Oasis. Your friends and family are relieved and happy to hear that you're slowly recovering."

A longing groan escaped my lips, "Why don't they come to see me?"

The new doctor shook his head, "They can't. Nobody knows the exact location of this place."

Frustration surged through me, and I shouted, "Why don't they use aircraft for reconnaissance? Why doesn't the army intervene?"

The doctor sighed, a helpless expression on his face. "The leader here has issued a dire warning. Any attempts to locate them without permission will result in a massacre, targeting all inhabitants near the oasis in the Sande Desert."

The air seemed to leave my lungs as I processed this revelation. Could the woman we were searching for truly issue such a ruthless order? It seemed implausible.

The doctor leaned closer, voice hushed. "Do you know? The leader of this tribe is a woman."

I nodded weakly, "I know."

He continued in an even lower tone, "She's known to be merciless, a bloodthirsty maniac who wouldn't hesitate to order a massacre. Her followers are all skilled swordsmen."

My lips trembled as I struggled to find words. After a long silence, I managed to ask, "Then why am I still alive? Why did she allow you to save me?"

The doctors exchanged glances, bewilderment in their eyes. "Who knows what goes on in the mind of such a formidable woman?" one replied.

My voice faltered, "Have you seen this leader?"

Both shook their heads in unison. The lack of answers left me stunned and silent, grappling with the mystery of her motives.

From that day forward, my condition gradually improved. Knowing that my family and friends were gathered at Yali Oasis fueled my desire to recover and reunite with them. Though my injuries healed slowly, I felt the strength of life returning little by little.

The two doctors devoted themselves to my care, and their efforts bore fruit. Two weeks later, I could see the scar on my stomach, a reminder of my ordeal, but it no longer appeared as menacing. It was just another mark of survival.

Pengdu remained a constant presence, watching over my progress. When I managed to stand and take a few steps with the aid of a cane, he asked with a curious smile, "You could have won that sword fight. Why did you suddenly stop?"

I offered a wry smile, shaking my head in response. The truth was complicated, tied to the unexpected recognition of the leader's identity.

"Did you not expect our leader to be a beautiful girl?" he continued, probing for an answer.

I shook my head again, and as Pengdu pressed on, I finally conceded, "I had seen her before. I came to the Sande Desert to find her, but I didn't expect to meet her in such a way."

His eyes widened in surprise, clearly intrigued but unsure how to proceed. I wasn't ready to reveal everything, and I seized the moment to ask, "Do you know why your leader spared my life?"

Pengdu paused, considering his response. "You had a chance to win," he said. "If she killed you after that, she would lose her right to be leader."

I nodded slowly, understanding the unspoken code of honor that governed their ways. "I see. But now that I'm healed, why am I still not allowed to leave?"

Pengdu shrugged, a smile playing on his lips. "That's not for me to decide. I'm sure the leader will meet with you eventually. You can ask her then."

Frustration flared within me. "When will she see me?" I demanded, my voice rising despite my weakened state. The exertion left me dizzy, and I sank back into my seat, my question hanging unanswered.

In the days that followed, my care improved further. A new doctor, arriving from Yali Oasis, provided comprehensive treatment, and the first doctor was released. This new physician brought news of Yali Oasis, telling me my wife, Flora, had arrived soon after my capture. Knowing that my gradual recovery had been communicated to them brought some relief and peace of mind.

My mood lifted, and with it, my recovery accelerated. After another fortnight, I could walk unaided, although I remained under constant watch. My movement was restricted to a few interconnected caves, and the outside world remained off-limits.

As the month drew to a close and I regained my strength, frustration mounted. Despite repeated requests, I had yet to meet the leader again. The anticipation of the encounter gnawed at me, and with each passing day, the desire to leave grew stronger.

It was time to devise a plan to reclaim my freedom and seek the answers I so desperately needed.

I was confident that I could find a way to escape, but the thought of leaving the two doctors behind troubled me. Their fate, should I disappear, was a concern I couldn't ignore. Moreover, the mystery of the leader intrigued me; I wasn't quite ready to leave without understanding her motives.

Days passed, and I felt my strength returning. Then, unexpectedly, Pengdu entered the cave, accompanied by two young women. This was unusual. Women rarely entered this space, and their presence immediately piqued my curiosity.

The women, though clad in traditional Arab attire, carried themselves with grace, their figures discernible beneath the fabric. Their uncovered faces and the unusual circumstances prompted me to ask, "What's the matter?"

Pengdu approached, his demeanor serious and almost conspiratorial. "Mr. Morris, the leader has summoned you."

The news was both a relief and a source of anxiety. The girl Mateo and I had set out to find, who we imagined as pure and gentle, was revealed to be the formidable leader of a tribe living by banditry. Her reputation, as conveyed by the doctor, was one of ruthlessness. Facing her again, I was unsure of my emotions.

Pengdu continued before I could respond, "Please follow these two girls. They are the chief's attendants."

With nothing left to say, I nodded, "Okay, please lead the way."

The two girls exchanged a glance, smiled, and turned to lead the way.

As I followed them out of the cave, the sunlight hit me with unexpected intensity. Having been deprived of natural light for nearly three months, the sun's glare was almost unbearable, forcing me to squint against its brilliance.

The girls moved briskly, and as we passed others, I noticed their peculiar stares, as if I were an anomaly in their midst. Near the pool, women paused in their tasks to gaze at me, heightening the sense of being an outsider.

The girls led me to a smaller cave, where a trickle of water flowed through a pipe. To my surprise, a complete set of washing tools awaited me. The girls pointed at the items, smiling, though they remained silent.

Their gestures were clear; they wanted me to wash and prepare before meeting the leader. I understood the importance of the ritual, both as a sign of respect and a step towards whatever awaited in this encounter. The prospect of finally seeing her again, under such circumstances, filled me with a mix of anticipation and trepidation.

I gazed at my reflection in the mirror, noting the transformation. It took me around half an hour to tame my hair and shave off the unruly beard. Although my face remained pale and gaunt, I looked much more like my former self. Satisfied, I turned to the two Arab girls, who gently draped a white robe over me, its fabric cool and comforting.

They guided me along a narrow mountain path, its confines making way to a refreshing coolness—a rare sensation in the desert. This oasis of relief was due to the cave's location deep within the mountain's embrace.

Emerging from the path, I found myself in a spacious cave, approximately twenty feet square. Yellow curtains surrounded the space, and at its center stood a large stone, neatly covered with felt. In each corner of the cave blazed braziers, their flames flickering and casting shifting shadows that lent an air of mystery to the setting.

The girls led me into the cave before retreating, leaving me alone in the flickering light. I waited, anticipation building, until the yellow curtain behind the stone lifted, and she appeared.

She had clearly adorned herself for the occasion. A crown-like headpiece, studded with fiery rubies, graced her head, and her white dress flowed elegantly as she emerged. She paused momentarily upon entering, then continued forward until she stood by the stone.

When she stopped, she smiled warmly at me. "Your injury has healed," she said, her voice carrying genuine warmth. "I am very happy!"

Her English, while slightly stiff, was remarkably clear and pure, her lovely voice making it sound natural and melodic.

I remained silent, absorbing the moment. She smiled again, seemingly unbothered by my silence. "I have never left the desert," she explained, "Pengdu taught me to speak English. Am I speaking well?"

Her question, filled with a touch of pride and vulnerability, broke the ice. Her presence was both commanding and gentle, a leader with an unexpected grace. I nodded, finding my voice. "Yes," I replied. "Your English is very good. I'm impressed."

The exchange marked a turning point, a moment where the boundaries between captor and captive blurred, allowing for a connection that transcended the situation. In her eyes, I saw both strength and curiosity, and the realization dawned that our meeting was as significant for her as it was for me.

I spoke calmly, "My injury has healed, and now I want to leave here."

She continued to look at me, and after a pause, she replied, "Yes, I know you have many friends waiting for you at Yali Oasis. Your wife is there too. She's very lovely."

Surprised, I asked, "You've seen her?"

"Of course," she laughed, a hint of pride in her smile. "In the desert, I am elusive, and no one recognizes me."

She went on, "I've been to Yali Oasis several times and even spoken with your wife. She seemed very anxious, hoping for your return."

I nodded, reinforcing my point, "That's exactly why I'm eager to leave."

She lowered her head briefly before saying, "I think you may not be able to go back. You also have to become one of us."

Her words were hesitant, her expression strange. But the implication that I couldn't return sparked a visceral reaction. I leapt to my feet, bypassing the nuances of her demeanor. "What did you say? You won't allow me to go back? Who do you think you are to detain someone at your whim?"

Her demeanor remained calm as she declared, "I am Princess Corona. My ancestors have ruled the Sande Desert for generations. Even now, I am the invisible master of this desert!"

I sneered defiantly, "I must leave. I don't care whether you allow it or not. I will leave!"

A coldness settled over her features. "Under my rule are over 200 first-class knifemen."

"Is that a threat?" I challenged.

She shook her head, "No, just a reminder."

I scoffed, "Given the crimes you and your family have committed, you all should spend the rest of your lives in prison. Enough talk. I'm leaving!"

Her expression hardened further, "You can't leave!"

I shouted, "What are you going to do?"

She stood resolute, the authority in her gaze unyielding. In that tense moment, the air between us crackled with unresolved conflict. Her calm demeanor belied the power she wielded, and though my resolve was firm, I understood the gravity of my situation. Her words were not mere threats; they were a reflection of the reality I was up against.

What Princess Corona said next was beyond anything I could have imagined.

Her smile was enigmatic, her motives hidden beneath an inscrutable expression. I couldn't help but wonder what lay behind that smile.

Then she spoke, "The wedding will be held tomorrow night, and everything has been prepared according to tradition."

For a moment, her words left me stunned, my impatience bubbling to the surface as I managed to ask, "Whose wedding?"

"Mine!" Princess Corona answered, her smile widening with a mysterious charm. She paused, letting her words sink in before adding, "With you!"

Her three words lingered in the air, their meaning slowly unfurling in my mind. "Me and you." The realization struck me like a bolt of lightning—she was speaking of marriage. Our marriage.

In that instant, my palms grew clammy, and my heart pounded fiercely. This was no jest; she was deadly serious.

I stood there, grappling with disbelief as her words echoed in my mind. "Are you kidding me? You and I? Marry? Are you kidding me?" I exclaimed, my voice tinged with incredulity.

Princess Corona's response was a gentle, almost serene smile, her demeanor unshaken by my outburst. Even amidst the tension, her smile remained captivating, an unsettling contrast to the situation.

"Don't laugh," I insisted, my voice rising. "This is impossible!"

Still smiling, she explained, "But I must have a husband, and my husband must possess greater swordsmanship than I do. Only you fit that description. I repeat, our wedding will be held tomorrow night."

Frustration boiled over, and I clenched my fists. "There will be no wedding!"

Her smile finally faded, replaced by a chilling calm. Her beauty took on a hard edge, her eyes cold and unyielding, like stones carved from ice. It was then that I began to understand the doctor's description of her as a bloodthirsty maniac, a term I'd previously questioned but could now see as less of an exaggeration.

"What do you want?" she asked, her voice steady.

Without hesitation, I replied, "To leave here!"

Her expression hardened further, the air growing colder around us. She regarded me with those stone-like eyes, her silence heavy with unspoken threats. "You can leave," she finally said.

Relief flooded through me, and I quickly responded, "Okay, goodbye then!"

But her sneer stopped me short. "Of course, not leaving like that. You will be taken to the center of the desert, and I will cut off your hands. If you can still support yourself in the desert and walk for three days and three nights, only then will you be naturally rescued."

Her words were like a death sentence, freezing the blood in my veins. I trembled, my mind struggling to process her cruel ultimatum. The harsh reality was undeniable—no one could survive such an ordeal. To wander the desert, handless and alone, was a certain death sentence, each step draining the life with each drop of blood.

As my body shook with anger and fear, Corona's cold words echoed in the cave, "Think about it yourself!"

I took a deep breath, my mind racing. Despite the dire situation, I knew I could never agree to such a marriage. I had a wife waiting for me, and even without that commitment, marrying under these circumstances was unthinkable. Even Mateo, who had been captivated by her photograph, would surely recoil upon learning the true nature of the woman before us.

I forced myself to think rationally, suppressing the anger that threatened to overwhelm me. "Usually, marriage is considered a major life event," I said, striving for a calm tone. "I need time to think about it."

Corona's response was icy, "If you need to consider marrying me, it is an insult to me. Insulting the leader is punished by having your eyes gouged out. Are you willing to accept that punishment?"

Her words were a chilling reminder of her authority and ruthlessness. My restraint snapped, and I cursed her, "Who are you, damn it? You're a bandit leader, a bloodthirsty criminal who should be hanged. I should kill you with one strike!"

A strange coldness glinted in Corona's eyes. She didn't retaliate with words or anger, but her gaze alone silenced me, its icy intensity more effective than any retort.

Breathing heavily, I met her gaze. After a long, tense silence, she spoke again, "You can go back. The wedding will be held tomorrow night."

With that, she clapped her hands twice, summoning two women into the cave. In that moment, a desperate plan formed in my mind. If I could subdue Corona, perhaps I could end this charade and escape.

As the women approached, I acted on impulse. I lunged forward, closing the distance between us in an instant. My hand shot out, aiming to seize her wrist and twist it behind her back, hoping to use her as leverage to secure my freedom.

The move was bold and reckless, driven by the urgent need to escape the trap she had laid. I knew the risks were high, but the prospect of regaining control over my fate spurred me into action, determined to end the farce and find a way back to the life that awaited me beyond the desert's grasp.

The air crackled with tension as Corona's body suddenly recoiled, her movements almost serpentine in their fluidity. Before I could process the shift, a blinding light exploded in my vision, halting my outstretched hand in its tracks.

In a heartbeat, the lethal arc of a scimitar sliced through the air, its gleaming edge poised precisely at my wrist. The blade whispered against my skin — a testament to its deadly sharpness—and I knew, with a jolt of primal fear, that a fraction more force would have severed my hand clean from my wrist.

Yet, Corona wielded her weapon with the precision of a master, withdrawing the blade at the exact moment contact was made. This was not luck; it was skill, honed to perfection. She truly was the preeminent knifeman of our age.

Paralyzed by the precariousness of the situation, I stood rigid, unsure whether to retract my hand. Corona mirrored my stillness, her gaze locked onto mine with an intensity that froze the air between us.

The silence stretched into an awkward tableau, my skin prickling with cold sweat. Corona's lips curled into a mocking smile, her voice dripping with derision. "Think you can outmaneuver me? Think again."

As I steadied my breath, trying to calm the storm within, Corona's focus shifted with the precision of a predator. Her gaze locked onto the two Arab women at the edge of the unfolding drama. "Come here!" Her voice was a blade, slicing cleanly through the palpable tension.

In a heartbeat, their expressions morphed into masks of fear, a sudden and inexplicable transformation that contrasted sharply with their prior calm. Their feet seemed rooted, unwilling to comply, until Corona's voice cracked like a whip, rising in both pitch and insistence. "Come here! Quickly!"

The two women stepped forward with trepidation, each movement calculated, their faces pale and reminiscent of alabaster masks. The air thickened with tension as Corona's gaze turned frostier. "What did you see just now?" she demanded, her voice an icy monotone that sent shivers down my spine.

Almost as if rehearsed, they responded in unison, their voices quivering with fear, "Nothing, nothing!"

Corona's laugh was a low, mocking sound. "You're not blind. How can you claim to see nothing?"

Their composure shattered further, their bodies now trembling visibly. Corona pressed on, her words laced with menace. "Only the blind see nothing. Only the blind believe in seeing nothing, isn't that right?"

Their lips barely moved as they muttered, "Yes."

In that moment, my mind was a whirl of confusion and burgeoning anger, unable to predict the unfolding events. The scimitar remained poised against my wrist, a constant reminder of the peril that surrounded me. My thoughts churned with revulsion, a deep-seated disgust that defied description.

No sooner had the word "yes" escaped their lips than Corona's demeanor shifted. "Okay!" she proclaimed, the word carrying a sinister finality.

With a swift, fluid motion, Corona's arm became a blur of deadly precision. The flash of her blade was followed by the piercing screams of the women. I turned quickly, my eyes drawn to the gruesome tableau.

Their faces bore the evidence of Corona's formidable skill—a single, precise cut traversed from the left corner of their eyes to the right. Blood cascaded down, mingling with their tears, marking them irrevocably blind.

I couldn't fathom how Corona executed such a calculated strike, her expertise evident in the aftermath. Yet, my emotions eclipsed my thoughts; fury surged within me, igniting my blood with a fiery intensity.

My face must have mirrored my wrath, flushed with the heat of righteous anger. I bellowed, my voice raw and defiant, as Corona's scimitar swung towards me, its lethal point now my immediate peril.

Corona's expression shifted to a chilling, enigmatic smile, her eyes never leaving mine as she barked sharp commands into the cavernous silence. The sound of approaching footsteps echoed ominously, and with a fluid motion, she sheathed her blade. Four imposing figures surged into the room, and at her signal, two of them swiftly escorted the injured women away, while the remaining pair flanked me, their grip unyielding.

Corona's gaze was unwavering. "Remember, our wedding will be held tomorrow night," she declared, her voice a blend of threat and promise.

Before I could react, the two men at my sides tightened their hold, immobilizing me with their formidable strength.

My mind raced, but their grip was like iron, leaving me powerless to resist.

Instead of returning to the cavern, they led me to a new location—a stark, stone prison. The door closed behind me with a resounding thud, sealing me in darkness. The dim light cast long shadows, and I paced the confined space, my thoughts a tumult of confusion and dread.

It was clear that Corona harbored no affection for me. She was a dangerous enigma, a beautiful facade masking a heart steeped in madness. Yet, she insisted on marriage. Was it simply because I had bested her in our swordsmanship duel?

I struggled to calm the tempest within, my mind fixated on escape.

As I wrestled with my thoughts, a small window creaked open in the wooden door, revealing Pengdu's familiar face. He gazed at me silently for a long moment, then sighed, "The princess is the most beautiful woman in all of Arabia. She's like a celestial being, a beauty straight out of legend. And yet, you refuse her?"

Meeting his eyes, I replied, "You're right, she is as beautiful as a fairy, but don't you see? She's as vicious as a devil."

Pengdu shook his head, his expression thoughtful. "You misunderstand. Strength is what has allowed us to survive in the harsh desert. Without it, our tribe would have vanished long ago. It's not about good or evil; it's about survival."

I inhaled deeply, reminded that Pengdu was one of them, bound by the same ruthless code. Discussing morality with him was absurd.

I stopped abruptly, turning away from the small window with a huff of frustration. Pengdu's voice followed, insistent and urgent. "It wasn't the princess who sent me. I came on my own after hearing about your encounter with her. Don't be a fool, don't let pride cloud your judgment!"

I offered no reply, only a derisive chuckle. Pengdu sighed heavily, "The wedding is tomorrow night—"

His words barely registered before I spun back toward the door, my fists crashing against the wood in a futile attempt to vent my anger. The pain from the impact shot through my hands, sharp and unforgiving, but somehow it soothed the turmoil within. "Get out!" I shouted, voice echoing in the confined space.

To my surprise, Pengdu's voice dropped to a conspiratorial whisper. "Even if you plan to escape, do you think you can manage it like this? You're being reckless!"

His words halted me in my tracks, the truth of them cutting through my frustration. I had to admit, he was right. I was trapped, with little chance of finding a way out.

After a beat, I asked, "Then what should I do? Do you have any advice?"

"First, you need to placate the princess," Pengdu suggested.

I laughed bitterly at the thought. "That's easier said than done!"

"Indeed," Pengdu conceded. "But if you're willing to follow my lead, kneel before her, and kiss her toes, it might soften her resolve."

CHAPTER 6

FALLING INTO A TRAP

The room seemed to shrink around me as I grappled with Pengdu's suggestion. If Princess Corona were a figure I adored, the act might have held a twisted sort of romance. But the mere thought of kneeling before her, this murderer who had ignited such vehement hatred within me, was unthinkable.

I inhaled deeply, searching for an alternative. "Is there any other way?" I asked, desperation lacing my words.

Pengdu's response was almost incredulous. "What's wrong with you? Her feet are so cute, why don't you do it?"

His words left me momentarily speechless. Pengdu continued, "This is the only way. It's our tradition, symbolizing a man's complete submission to a woman. If you defy it, the true God will punish you. Only by doing this will the princess trust you, giving you a chance to escape."

I remained silent, the weight of the situation pressing down on me.

Pengdu's expression shifted to one of frustration. "Perhaps I'm wasting my breath. Maybe you actually want to marry the princess!"

"What are you talking about?" I snapped, my anger flaring.

He leaned closer, urgency in his voice. "Then why hesitate? If the princess believes in your loyalty, I can provide you with three camels, supplies of water, and food. If you find anyone within three days, you'll be safe, beyond the reach of divine punishment."

His insistence left me momentarily dazed. Why was Pengdu so eager to aid me?

"Why are you so invested in this?" I asked, suspicion creeping into my voice.

"For myself," Pengdu replied quietly.

"For yourself?" I echoed, perplexed.

"I'm the princess's cousin. If she remains unmarried by her 21st birthday, I become her husband," he explained with a rapid urgency.

"Then just kill me," I replied, the edge in my tone unmistakable.

Pengdu shook his head. "I've received higher education. Remember that."

Realizing the depth of his predicament, I nodded, steeling myself for what lay ahead. "Alright, take me to her. I'll show my loyalty."

Pengdu stepped back, raising his voice to alert the guards. Only then did I notice the presence of others— eight guards, including the second knifeman I'd dueled.

In the dim glow of the desert sun, I trailed behind Pengdu, my thoughts a chaotic swirl of shame and resolve. I won't linger on the degradation I endured; suffice it to say, it was the most profound humiliation I had ever faced.

Yet, amidst this torment, one thing stood out sharply in my mind: Corona. Her beauty was undeniable, a striking figure of allure. As I knelt before her, she extended her foot with a regal grace, and when my lips brushed against her toes, I glimpsed her perfectly sculpted thighs. But despite her allure, my heart remained unmoved.

Pengdu was my silent ally. He led me away from that scene of disgrace, and as we exited, Corona's laughter — melodious and haunting — echoed in my ears.

We had plotted my escape with meticulous care. Pengdu, ever resourceful, had prepared all I needed: an escape route sketched in the sand, three sturdy camels, provisions of food and water. He advised that I flee two hours before the wedding, when the tribe would be swept up in festive delirium. The desert sun would have dipped below the horizon by then.

If I followed Pengdu's instructions precisely, racing through the night on camelback, I would reach a small oasis by dawn. From there, the path to the Yali Oasis would be clear and unchallenging.

To reassure me, Pengdu even took me on a moonlit inspection of the camels and supplies he had stashed away. Everything seemed set for a flawless escape. With Pengdu's guidance, freedom was within reach.

Yet, the anticipation gnawed at me like a relentless beast. The hours leading to my escape stretched interminably, each moment a test of my patience and resolve.

As custom demanded, I was prepared for the role of a bridegroom, my body oiled and garbed in a ceremonial robe.

Finally, dusk descended, painting the desert in hues of deep orange and purple. As the last rays of the sun vanished, bonfires sparked to life across the tribe's encampment. Laughter and music filled the air as the tribe surrendered to revelry—my signal to vanish into the night.

Anxiety clutched at my chest as I sat in the cave, each echoing drop of water a reminder of the passage of time. Then, like a shadow slipping into the room, Pengdu appeared. His presence was a balm to my nerves. He dismissed the attendants with a silent gesture, leaning in to whisper, "It's time. You know where the camels are."

I nodded, my voice steady despite the storm within. "I know."

"Ride the camel and follow the path I've laid out for you," he urged, his eyes holding mine with a fierce insistence.

I rose, my resolve as solid as the mountain walls around us. Together, we stepped into the night's embrace. The fires from the tribe's revelry flickered in the distance, casting long shadows on the sand. I shed the robe adorned with ceremonial ribbons, making my way along the rugged mountain edge to where the camels awaited.

With swift, practiced hands, I untied the reins, grasping those of two camels before mounting the third. The beast shifted beneath me as I urged it forward, the pace deliberate until we rounded the cliff's edge. Then, with a sharp slap, I spurred it into a gallop, the wind whipping past as the rhythm of the desert night engulfed me.

Within minutes, the encampment lights were swallowed by the vast, starlit darkness. A cry of triumph bubbled up within me—I was free!

Guided by the celestial map above, I kept to the direction Pengdu had whispered, the stars my silent companions.

The desert was a sea of silence, vast and profound, as I rode on through the night. Around midnight, I allowed myself a brief pause, the solitude of the sands enveloping me.

In that moment of stillness, my thoughts drifted back to Corona.

What would she do when she discovered my absence? Would her laughter still echo, or would it be replaced by a storm of fury?

Of course, Corona would be furious. If she discovered Pengdu's betrayal, his role as the architect of my escape, she'd undoubtedly exact her vengeance. Her fury would be swift and unforgiving.

I sighed, the weight of the situation settling heavily on my shoulders. Isn't it ironic? The mirage that once painted Corona as a vision of beauty now revealed her true nature—a tempest of violence and malice lurking beneath that captivating exterior.

Though I was tempted to push onward, eager to reach the safety of the civilized world, both the camels and I needed rest. The desert night demanded it.

I commanded the camels to kneel, their bodies providing a makeshift shelter against the chill. I nestled between them, sipping the water Pengdu had packed for me, its taste carrying an unfamiliar tang. In the barren expanse of the desert, I couldn't afford the luxury of being choosy. I ate some of the dry food, also thoughtfully prepared by Pengdu, and tried to calm my racing thoughts.

The silence was profound, a deep, enveloping quiet that pressed down on me. Despite my excitement and the adrenaline coursing through my veins, I forced myself to rest. Without sleep, I would lack the strength needed to traverse the relentless desert.

As I began to succumb to exhaustion, a distant shout pierced the stillness. In the crisp, arid air, the sound was disturbingly clear. My heart skipped a beat. They were coming—at least dozens of them—and they were less than half a mile away.

Panic surged through me, and I scrambled to my feet, startling the camels into uneasy shifts. But as I rose, a wave of dizziness crashed over me. My vision blurred, and my limbs felt like lead.

I tried to steady myself, pressing my hands into the sand to stand, but weakness spread through my body like a poison.

In a moment of sheer panic, I was frozen, unable to comprehend the sudden weakness that gripped my limbs. The pounding noise of approaching pursuers grew louder, yet I remained crumpled on the desert sand, struggling to rise. My mind raced—how could this be? My wounds had healed, my strength restored. Yet here I was, powerless.

Desperation clawed at me as I collapsed to my knees, the cacophony of voices drawing nearer, their torches flickering like specters in the night. They were Corona 's men, dispatched to hunt me down, and I was at their mercy.

In my helpless state, I couldn't fathom the cause of my sudden frailty. I needed to escape, to climb onto the camel and flee, but my body betrayed me.

The cacophony of voices encroached ever closer, their torches illuminating the night like fiery beacons of impending doom. My heart pounded in my chest as I realized there was no escape, no chance to flee.

In a desperate bid for survival, I collapsed onto the desert floor, mustering every ounce of strength to kick the camels into motion. They lurched forward, carrying the precious cargo of food and water—my lifeline in this barren expanse.

Yet, in the vast openness of the desert, they were conspicuous targets. With a heavy heart, I sent them away, a silent prayer on my lips that their movement would draw attention away from me. I pressed myself into the sand, hoping to remain unseen.

As I lay there, the chaotic symphony of voices began to scatter, like leaves caught in a sudden gust of wind. My head felt leaden, a dull throb clouding my thoughts. Forcing myself to lift it, I peered into the distance. Torches danced in the night, more than a dozen splitting into two groups, moving rapidly away.

Yet one torch diverged from the others, coming straight toward me. Why was this person different? Fear gripped me anew. Would they discover me lying here?

As the lone figure approached, it became clear they were headed directly for me, as if they knew my precise location. The rider dismounted, and a glint of steel caught my eye—a knife, poised and ready.

Despair overwhelmed me, but then the torch illuminated the rider's face. "Pengdu!" I gasped, recognizing my ally.

My tension melted away at the sight of him, replaced by a rush of relief. "Pengdu, you've saved me. Did you send the others away? Help me onto the camel. We must leave!"

Pengdu lowered the torch, concern etched on his face. "What's wrong with you?" he asked.

"I don't know," I replied, my voice shaky. "Suddenly, I have no strength. Did Corona suspect your involvement?"

He chuckled softly, shaking his head. "No, she didn't. Let's get you on the camel."

With deft hands, he sheathed the knife into the sand, lifting me with care onto his camel. I lay across its back, the world spinning around me. "Which direction should I go?" I asked, my voice barely a whisper.

Pengdu's words struck me like a thunderclap. "I'll take you back," he repeated, his voice a chilling echo in the night air.

For a moment, I thought I must have misheard. "What?" I stammered, my mind struggling to process the betrayal.

But Pengdu's response was unyielding. "Let's go back!" he insisted, his eyes cold and determined.

Fear coursed through me, leaving a trail of ice in its wake. My voice trembled as I asked, "You—you're not joking, are you?"

Pengdu's hand moved to the scimitar embedded in the sand, pulling it free with a decisive motion. "No," he replied, his tone devoid of empathy.

Panic gripped me, sweat beading on my forehead. "You — you — you took me away!" I protested, desperation creeping into my voice.

Pengdu remained silent, the weight of his betrayal settling heavily between us. I clung to a sliver of hope, reminding him, "Pengdu, you said that if I escaped, you could marry Corona!"

He met my gaze, a cruel smile playing on his lips. "Yes," he conceded, "but I forgot to mention one detail: I must capture the fugitive alive. Only then will Corona marry me."

His words pierced me like daggers, each one a testament to his treachery. I had been deceived, led into a trap by someone I thought an ally. Pengdu, a man of education and cunning, was far more dangerous than any common bandit. He had orchestrated my escape, only to ensure my capture.

The water I drank—the strange taste—it all made sense now. I had been drugged, rendered weak and defenseless. Pengdu had played me perfectly.

In a surge of defiance, I shouted, "Do you think I won't tell Corona the truth?"

Pengdu's laughter was a dark melody. "First, Corona is furious and won't believe you. Second, you won't have the chance to speak. Do you understand? No chance!"

A chill washed over me. "What do you mean?" I demanded.

"When we are close," Pengdu said, his voice low and menacing, "I will cut your throat. You won't be able to speak at all." He brandished the knife near my throat for emphasis. "Not now, of course. If I did it now, you'd bleed out before we reached her. I need you alive, so Corona can kill you herself. That's how I win."

Rage surged through me like a storm, yet words failed to form. My throat constricted with unspoken curses, unable to convey the depth of my fury at Pengdu's betrayal. All I could do was glare at him, my eyes burning with silent condemnation, as he led the camel onward.

I lay draped over the camel's back, each step a reminder of my helplessness, the drug-induced weakness coursing through my veins. Pengdu's plan was painfully clear: deliver me to Corona, where death awaited like a dark promise.

Despair clawed at my heart, dragging it into an abyss of inevitability. I was going to die. Never before had the specter of death felt so tangible, its icy fingers wrapping around my very being.

As Pengdu guided the camel forward, he soon realized our pace was too slow. He commanded the camel to kneel, mounting it with practiced ease. With a swift pat, we lurched into motion, the desert landscape blurring past in a rush of sand and shadow.

The faster we rode, the closer I came to my grim fate. Yet, somewhere deep within, a primal instinct flared to life—a desperate urge to survive. I couldn't surrender, not without a fight. My will to live surged forth, igniting a fire in my veins.

To my astonishment, strength began to seep back into my limbs. My heart pounded with renewed vigor, and sensation returned to my fingers. I realized then that Pengdu must have laced the water with something to debilitate me. But I had drunk sparingly, conserving what little I had for the uncertain journey ahead. This, coupled with the fierce determination that now burned within me, was counteracting the drug's effects.

My mind latched onto this glimmer of hope, clinging to it as a lifeline. The more I focused on survival, the more my body responded. The fog of weakness lifted, replaced by a clarity of purpose. I would not be led to slaughter without a struggle. I would fight for every breath, every heartbeat, until the very end.

The camel thundered across the desert, its hooves pounding against the sand, as the shadow of a looming cliff came into view. Time was slipping away, and I couldn't afford to hesitate any longer. Whatever strength had returned to me had to be enough.

In a sudden surge of determination, I twisted my body, my hands finding their grip on Pengdu's collar. With a forceful motion, I straightened and rolled off the camel's saddle, dragging Pengdu down with me.

We tumbled across the desert floor, a chaotic whirl of limbs and sand. Pengdu's roar of surprise shattered the silence of the night as he broke free and sprang to his feet. Before I could even react, a sharp kick landed on my face, and my vision exploded into a constellation of stars.

Despite the pain, I instinctively clutched the foot he hadn't yet retracted, yanking hard. Pengdu toppled backward, hitting the ground with a thud. Seizing the moment, I grabbed a fistful of sand and flung it into his eyes, blinding him.

Pengdu's scimitar flashed in the dim light as he swung it wildly, narrowly missing me. I knew I couldn't hold him forever; his strength and fury were formidable. Yet, I couldn't afford to let him go, knowing he would end my life in a heartbeat.

In the chaos, I lifted his foot, and as his blade arced through the air, his own misjudged swing severed his right foot. The scream he unleashed was a sound I'll never forget—a mix of agony and disbelief.

Blood pooled in the sand as Pengdu writhed, and I scrambled to regain my footing. The camel had halted nearby, and I crawled to it, grasping the reins. With a pull, the camel knelt, and I hauled myself onto its saddle.

The camel rose, and I directed it away from the scene of our struggle. I clung to its back, every muscle trembling with exertion, sweat pouring down my face. I had no sense of direction, only a primal urge to distance myself from the bandits and the treacherous sands.

For an hour, the camel carried me through the night, the rhythmic gait steadying my racing heart. Slowly, clarity returned, the fog of exhaustion lifting. As strength seeped back into my limbs, I realized I had survived.

I managed to sit upright on the camel's back, surveying the vast, gray-white expanse of desert that stretched to the horizon in every direction. The camel plodded forward at a languid pace, but I dared not halt its progress. Thirst clawed at my throat, a relentless gnawing that worsened with the rising sun.

As the day wore on, my thirst intensified, each breath a rasping struggle. My lips, crusted with sand and a strange salty residue, cracked painfully as I licked them. Desperation gnawed at the edges of my mind as I dismounted. The thought crossed my mind — my survival could hinge on the camel. Drinking its blood might stave off the immediate threat of dehydration.

Yet, the thought of sacrificing the camel filled me with dread. The desert stretched endlessly around me, a barren sea of sand with no oasis in sight. Once the camel was gone, so too would be my lifeline. Facing the second wave of thirst on foot would be a death sentence.

I coaxed the camel to its feet and crouched beneath its belly, seeking refuge from the sun's merciless rays. My mind raced, searching for a solution. Though I had escaped Pengdu's grasp, the desert itself felt like a more insidious captor, its shadow of death a constant presence.

Minutes ticked by, each one an eternity. My thirst grew exponentially, a cruel reminder of my dire situation. Not a single drop of water to be found—my parched body cried out for relief that would not come.

Realizing I couldn't remain there indefinitely, I climbed back onto the camel, its steady gait my only hope. Each second felt eternal, the sun a relentless sentinel overhead. My consciousness wavered under its oppressive heat, and time dragged on in agonizing increments.

In the haze of near-unconsciousness, I clung to the camel, the passage of time marked by the slow arc of the sun.

As darkness finally draped its soothing cloak over the desert, I realized with a start that I had somehow endured the day. The moon cast a silver glow across the endless sands, a stark reminder of the isolation that surrounded me.

With no other choice, I slid off the camel's back, the weight of my decision heavy on my shoulders. To survive, I would have to make the ultimate sacrifice—the camel, my last companion in this desolate expanse. My body screamed for water, each parched cell echoing a desperate plea: Water—water—!

Yet, there was none to be had. My blood felt thick and sluggish, unable to sustain my fading life. In the moonlight, I drew out a small knife I had concealed, ready to do what was necessary to survive another day.

But just as resolve hardened within me, the camel, as if sensing its impending fate, sprang to its feet and bolted. I watched, dumbfounded, as it disappeared into the night, a fleeting shadow against the moonlit sands. Perhaps it was a primal instinct, a sixth sense driving it to preserve its own life.

Staring into the vast emptiness, I was paralyzed by a crushing sense of loss. My last hope vanished with the camel's retreating form. The specter of death loomed larger, whispering promises of an end to suffering.

I turned the small knife over in my hands, its blade glinting under the moon's gaze. Though only an inch long, it was sharp enough to sever the thin thread of my existence. The question loomed, heavy and insistent: Do I take control of my fate and end it now, or do I cling to the slimmest thread of hope and wait for dawn?

In that moment of profound solitude, the decision hung in the balance, a testament to the indomitable human spirit and its endless struggle against despair.

CHAPTER 7

———

CONFRONTING EVIL

Desperation clung to me like the desert sand, and my mind clung to fragile hopes that the next oasis might be just over the next rise, perhaps a mere mile away. Perhaps, with a few more steps, I could escape this barren grave and find sanctuary. It was the same mirage of hope that has driven countless souls to crawl onward, their bodies eventually claimed by the sands, forever frozen in their final, desperate lunge toward life.

Such is the cruel irony of the desert—a place where hope and despair dance a perilous waltz. Watching others succumb to this illusion, one might scoff at their folly. Yet, when faced with the same desolate expanse,

I found myself echoing their struggle, one faltering step at a time.

With legs that ached and feet that stumbled over each other, I pushed forward. Every step drained what little strength remained, until my body could bear no more and collapsed onto the unforgiving ground.

Even then, I refused to surrender. I began to crawl, dragging my weary frame inch by inch, my elbows carving a path through the sand. But eventually, even that meager progress became impossible. Exhausted, I lay still, staring into the infinite stretch of moonlit desert. It was a haunting beauty, the serene and silent promise of death.

I closed my eyes, surrendering to the abyss. Time slipped away, and when I finally opened them again, a surreal sight met my gaze. A figure on camelback emerged from the horizon, a solitary silhouette against the vast backdrop of night. They were moving toward me.

I blinked rapidly, trying to clear my vision, disbelief clouding my senses. Yes, a man on a camel was indeed approaching. I let out a hoarse shout, but doubt gnawed at the edges of my mind. Was this a mirage? Could the moonlight conjure such illusions?

Pushing the thought aside, I forced myself upright, swaying but standing nonetheless. The camel rider drew near, halting before me, his identity unmistakable. An Arab, his features blurred in my exhausted gaze, but his presence undeniable. My heart screamed for water, but my parched throat could only emit a rasping whisper, a sound like dry leaves rustling in the wind.

He dismounted, pulling the scarf from his head, and his voice cut through the night air with an icy clarity. "I finally found you!"

Recognition hit me like a blow. It was Corona.

I crumpled to the sand, powerless to do anything but gaze at her. Her eyes bore into me with a chilling indifference, as if savoring my plight. She laughed, a sharp, mocking sound that echoed around us. "Run away? I don't need to kill you anymore. Your fate is sealed."

Again, my throat convulsed, struggling to form words. "Give me... water," I rasped, the plea barely audible.

Corona's sneer deepened as her foot connected with my face. My lips, parched and cracked, couldn't even cling to the sand. She turned back to her camel, reaching for a leather bag that sloshed tantalizingly with water. My heart surged with hope at the sound, and I managed to croak, "Give it to me!"

She looked down at me with disdain. "And if I do, what will you do?"

My lips quivered, unable to form a coherent reply. But she stepped forward, unstopped the bag, and tilted it toward me. I drank deeply, savoring the life-giving liquid, each drop a balm to my ravaged throat.

Yet, after only two mouthfuls, she withdrew it. "Now tell me, what will you do to me?" she demanded.

The water, scant as it was, ignited a spark of strength within me. Though my thirst was far from sated, it gave me enough vigor to stand once more. I fixed my gaze on her, my resolve hardening.

"Give me more," I asked, my voice steadier.

Corona's voice sharpened, her question slicing the air. "I ask you again, how will you treat me?"

Summoning every ounce of will, I rose to my feet, my stare unwavering. Something in my eyes must have unnerved her, for she took a step back. Her retreat was all the encouragement I needed. In that instant, my plan formed with the clarity of lightning, and I lunged forward to seize the leather bag.

Corona's scream pierced the night as I wrenched it from her grasp. Her nails raked my face, but pain was inconsequential now. The leather bag—my salvation—was in my hands.

Turning, I sprinted away, fumbling with the stopper to unleash the precious water within. Each step carried me farther from Corona, each drop a promise of survival. In the moonlit desert, with the taste of water still on my lips, hope surged anew.

The sound of a blade slicing through the air behind me sent a jolt of adrenaline coursing through my veins. Instinctively, I dropped to the ground, rolling away and kicking up a cloud of sand to obscure Corona's vision.

As I hit the ground, the leather bag slipped from my grasp, spilling water onto the desert floor. Desperation drove me to press my lips against it, gulping down what I could before it was lost. Each drop was a lifeline, a fleeting taste of survival.

The sand I kicked up forced Corona to halt, but only momentarily. She charged forward again, her scimitar poised to strike. With nothing but the torn leather bag in my hands, I raised it reflexively in defense. The blade flashed under the moonlight, and with a swift slash, the bag was cleaved open, dousing me in its precious contents.

I sprang to my feet, savoring the last gulps of water, expecting her assault to continue. Yet, to my surprise, Corona stood rooted, knife in hand, but making no move to advance.

I took a moment to catch my breath, invigorated by the water. The emptiness within me was filled, the fatigue lifting like a fog. Wielding the empty leather bag as a makeshift weapon, I prepared to defend myself, but she remained still, her eyes fixed on something beyond me.

Then, without warning, she screamed—a sound of raw frustration—and dashed toward her camel. In her haste, she neglected to sheath the scimitar, and its edge grazed the camel's side. The startled beast reared back, neck stretched high, before bolting into the desert, dragging Corona along the ground.

She struggled to her feet, her face now a mask of helpless rage. The camel, now a distant silhouette, was her escape—and mine—vanishing into the night.

Corona's gaze turned to me, her expression a twisted blend of fury and despair. "You beast!" she spat, her voice filled with venom.

I met her stare with cold detachment, confused by the depth of her anger. She still held the blade, the apparent victor, yet her fury was palpable, as if I had torn her world asunder.

In that moment, I realized it wasn't just the loss of the camel that enraged her, but the unraveling of her control, the shattering of her plans. Her world, once meticulously constructed, had crumbled, leaving her stranded in the very desert she sought to command.

I stared at her, trying to decipher the layers of emotion etched on her face. Then she laughed again, an unsettling sound that echoed in the stillness of the desert. "Okay! This time, we will all die in the desert!" she declared, her voice tinged with madness.

Her words hit me like a blow. "Die in the desert?" I echoed, disbelief mingling with the remnants of fear.

Corona's voice rose, sharp and piercing. "Yes, it takes four days to reach the nearest water source on foot. Can you or I survive without water for four days? And you wasted an entire bag!"

The reality of our predicament settled over me like a suffocating shroud. Though I had quenched my thirst for now, the memory of that desperate thirst clawed at my mind. The thought of another four days without water sent an involuntary shiver through my body.

It dawned on me why Corona had rushed to her camel after slashing the leather bag. With it, she could have reached the water source in less than four days. But now, with her camel gone, even this formidable queen of the desert was reduced to the same vulnerability as any mortal.

A strange amusement bubbled up inside me. Her fury, her helplessness—there was a peculiar irony in it all. I couldn't stop myself from laughing, the sound bitter yet liberating.

"Don't be angry, Miss," I said, a wry smile playing at my lips. "Anger only makes you thirstier. Perhaps it's best to embrace the inevitable sooner."

For a fleeting moment, a sense of peace washed over me. If I had to die, at least it wouldn't be by her hand. But my relief was tragically short-lived.

Corona's laughter rang out, a chilling melody of malevolence. Her beautiful features twisted into a smile that was anything but kind. A shiver danced down my spine.

"Go!" she commanded, the knife in her hand glinting under the moonlight, pointing the way forward.

I hesitated, trying to reason with her madness. "Why go further? Neither of us will last four days without water."

Corona's wicked smile deepened, her white teeth gleaming like a predator's under the moonlight. The malevolence in her expression was chilling, a prelude to the revelation that followed.

She spoke deliberately, her words dripping with malice. "Don't forget, I grew up in the desert. I have a special ability to endure thirst."

Her claim hung in the air, and I couldn't help but question it. "Can you go without water for four days?" I asked, skepticism threading through my voice.

Corona's eyes sparkled with a dangerous light, and her reply was disarmingly simple. "No, two days."

I almost dismissed her boast as bravado, but then it struck me—a realization that sent a shiver down my spine. I understood what Corona intended, and my entire body went numb with the knowledge.

She cackled, the sound sharp and piercing. "You should understand that I can reach the nearest water source as long as I don't drink water for two days. You understand, don't you?"

The chilling truth of her words settled over me. Her plan was diabolical. She would drive me forward for two days. When she could no longer endure the thirst, she would end my life and sustain herself on my blood, eking out two more days of survival until she reached the oasis.

It was the same desperate strategy I had considered for the camel, but now she intended to use it on me— a human being.

Corona's laughter echoed in the desert night, a sound that confirmed she knew I grasped her grim intention. With the knife in her hand, I was at her mercy, stripped of any hope of resistance.

Her laughter ceased abruptly, her voice turning steely. "Go!"

With a heavy heart, I turned and trudged forward, the weight of impending doom pressing down with every step. The desert stretched ahead, an endless expanse of sand and starlight, offering no refuge from the sinister reality that stalked close behind.

The desert stretched endlessly before me, each step a struggle through the soft, yielding sand. My legs felt disconnected from my body, driven only by the grim knowledge that my blood was the thread sustaining Corona's life.

The moon cast our shadows on the sand, a haunting tableau of predator and prey. Corona followed closely, never more than six feet behind, her presence an inescapable reminder of the peril shadowing my every move.

As the initial shock of our predicament subsided, my thoughts began to clear. I spoke, my voice breaking the silence. "If you've decided to kill me to sustain yourself, what makes you so sure I won't resist now?"

Corona's response was swift and sharp. "You won't, because if you resist now, you die now."

A bitter laugh escaped my lips. "And if I die, I'll take you with me."

But Corona only laughed, her voice laced with a dark certainty. "No, you have two days left to live. In those two days, you might find a way to change things. Hope keeps you from fighting me, from dying until I decide it's time."

Her words left me momentarily speechless.

"Pengdu once said," she continued, "that a tribesman called hope the biggest liar. Yet everyone lives under its deceit, clinging to life despite knowing their hopes may never come true. You are no exception."

Inwardly, I acknowledged the truth of her words. Hope, that cruel mirage, was what kept me moving, searching for a way out. The thought of wresting the scimitar from Corona flitted through my mind, a desperate fantasy. But even if I succeeded, the desert's brutal reality loomed large. I couldn't survive four days without water, but it was still preferable to dying by her hand.

A bitter smile tugged at my lips as I trudged on, the irony of my situation not lost on me. Hope, that relentless whisperer of lies, kept me from acting rashly.

The sand beneath my feet was deceptively soft, lulling me into a false sense of comfort with each step. But lifting my feet again was a Herculean effort, the fatigue settling deeply into my bones.

Corona's shadow remained constant, a specter of inevitability. My mind raced, seeking any possible avenue of escape, but the fatigue and fear dulled my thoughts, leaving me adrift in a sea of uncertainty.

As the night wore on, the oppressive weight of the desert pressed down on me, and I realized that, for now, all I could do was keep moving forward, step by step, clinging to the slender thread of hope that refused to let me go.

As the first light of dawn crept over the horizon, painting the desert in hues of gold and orange, the sun began its relentless climb into the sky. With it came the promise of another day's torment under its burning gaze.

The night's journey had been grueling, but the day would be far worse. The sun hung heavy above, a merciless overseer, its heat pressing down like a tangible weight. Each step forward became a monumental effort, my body straining with the exertion and the growing thirst gnawing at my insides.

As the sun reached its zenith, I could feel the moisture evaporating from my skin, leaving behind a sticky residue of salt and fatigue. My lips were parched, and each breath felt like inhaling hot smoke. Eventually, my strength gave out, and I collapsed onto the sand, my breath coming in ragged gasps.

Corona was on me in an instant, her foot connecting with my side, her voice a harsh torrent of words I couldn't comprehend. But her intent was clear — she was driving me onward, her curses punctuated by sharp kicks aimed at forcing me back to my feet.

"Don't force me!" I shouted, the words tearing at my sore throat. "Let me rest, just for a moment!"

Her response was a venomous command, "Get up, you beast! If you stop now, you'll never rise again!"

I groaned, the truth of her words a bitter pill. "Why should I care? I'll die by your hand regardless!"

But Corona, unyielding, retorted with steely resolve, "Keep moving, and you'll live at least one more day!"

Her words, harsh as they were, held a glimmer of truth that pierced the fog of despair. The promise of one more day, a single thread of time to grasp at hope, was enough to stir me into motion once more. With a monumental effort, I dragged myself to my feet.

Yes, one more day. For someone teetering on the brink of death, an extra day held immeasurable promise—a chance to turn the tide, to find a way out of this nightmare. With shaky resolve, I forced myself onward, one step at a time, clinging to the fragile hope that tomorrow might bring a change.

As I stood and looked at Corona, the transformation was stark and unsettling. In just twelve hours of crossing the desert, the harsh conditions had etched themselves onto her once smooth skin, which was now rough and peppered with salt crystals. Her lips were cracked and dry, and her eyes shone with a fierce intensity that was almost inhuman. The knife in her hand seemed to be an extension of her will, a tool of survival and dominance.

This person, who had once held an allure of beauty and mystery, now appeared as a relentless force of nature, driven by an unyielding desire to survive at any cost. The desert had stripped away any veneer of civility, revealing something raw and primal beneath.

I opted for silence, turning away and pressing forward. Words were futile for someone who had forsaken her humanity. Though she remained human in form, the desert's relentless gaze had twisted her into something unrecognizable.

With each step, I was acutely aware of her presence behind me, a constant reminder of the peril that lay in both the desert and the company I kept. The silence between us was heavy, filled with unspoken tensions and the shared understanding of the brutal reality we faced.

As the sun finally dipped below the horizon, casting the desert in shadows, I found myself collapsing for what felt like the umpteenth time. My body had reached its limit, exhaustion wrapping around me like a heavy shroud. Each fall had been met with kicks and curses from Corona, her relentless drive pushing us forward without pause. She seemed almost immune to the desert's toll, while I was utterly spent.

This time, no amount of her harsh encouragement could rouse me. I lay still, my body refusing to respond, while Corona, finally conceding to her own fatigue, dropped down beside me, her breath labored.

The darkness settled around us, the cool night air a stark contrast to the day's searing heat. I lifted my head after a long while, peering through the dim light at Corona. Her outline was indistinct, but her eyes pierced the gloom, sharp and dangerous.

A dry laugh bubbled up from within me, a sound tinged with irony and despair. "In this situation," I rasped, "even if you kill me, there's no guarantee you'll make it out of the desert alive."

The truth of my words hung between us, a sobering reminder of the stark reality we faced. The desert was an impartial adversary, indifferent to our struggles and intentions. It cared little whether we lived or perished beneath its vast, star-strewn canopy.

Her gaze was like daggers, and I laughed again, a sound tinged with madness. Her knife flashed as she raised it, the blade hovering threateningly close. But instead of striking, she halted, her voice cutting through the darkness. "Get up."

With effort, I pushed myself up, using the sand for support. Standing shakily, I faced her, the knife's tip a mere whisper from my chest. "I can't go any further. I'm at my limit. I'd rather die than keep pushing on."

Her response was cold, devoid of sympathy. "You were going to die anyway."

I took a deep breath, the knife a chilling reminder of how precarious my situation was. The desert stretched out around us, indifferent to our struggle, a vast expanse that promised nothing but more hardship.

Despite my desperation, the thought of seizing the knife from Corona was a futile fantasy. I knew that any attempt to snatch it could end disastrously, costing me my hand or worse. Resigned, I turned away and trudged forward, each step a monumental effort as my body teetered on the brink of collapse.

I had reached the very edge of my endurance. Every step sent tremors through my limbs, and I found myself collapsing to the ground every sixteen or seventeen steps. Rising each time became an ordeal, my body protesting every movement.

Corona must have noticed my diminishing strength. Her cruelty intensified as she used the knife to prick my back, sharp bursts of pain forcing me into a desperate, stumbling run. It was a brutal tactic, squeezing every last ounce of energy from me, driving me to continue forward like a cornered animal.

The night blurred into a haze of pain and exhaustion. I was no longer aware of time, only the relentless push to move.

When dawn finally broke, its first light spilled over the desert, and I crumpled to the ground, utterly spent. I could crawl no further; my strength was utterly depleted.

Corona, too, seemed to have reached her limit. She no longer commanded or prodded but simply stood, panting, the knife still in her grasp. We were both shadows of our former selves, the desert having stripped us of everything but the will to survive.

I lay there as the sun rose, its rays searing my skin, amplifying the pain that riddled my body. It was a pain so profound that, for the first time, the thought of death seemed a release. To escape the relentless torment, even through death, felt like a mercy.

With that acceptance came a strange, quiet peace. I lay motionless, eyes closed, waiting for the end to claim me.

In that moment, the struggle ceased, replaced by a tranquil resignation. Life, with all its suffering, faded into the background as I awaited the inevitable, the promise of pain's end offering a solace I never thought I'd seek.

The moment stretched out before me, a rare opportunity in the midst of despair. Corona stood with her back to me, her attention wholly absorbed by whatever lay ahead. The desert, usually so merciless, had granted me this singular chance to act.

Despite the oppressive heat and fatigue that clung to my limbs, the instinct to survive ignited within me. Slowly, carefully, I pushed myself up from the sand, the fire of determination burning away the remnants of exhaustion. Here was a chance to tilt the balance, to reclaim some semblance of control over my fate.

I moved with deliberate quiet, sand shifting silently underfoot as I approached the dune. My heart pounded in my chest, each beat echoing with the urgency of the moment. With Corona unaware and vulnerable, I knew I had to seize this chance decisively.

Summoning every last reserve of strength, I launched myself forward, tackling her with a force that belied my earlier weakness. We tumbled down the dune, a chaotic blur of movement and sand. Instinctively, I grabbed for her wrist and neck, wrestling the scimitar from her grasp. My knee pinned her, forcing her to release the weapon as we rolled apart.

I staggered to my feet, the knife now firmly in my hand. Corona kneeled in the sand, her eyes wide with shock and fear. The tables had turned; the power she once wielded was now mine.

For a moment, I hesitated, the weight of the scimitar heavy in my grasp. The primal urge for survival battled with the remnants of humanity within me. But before I could decide, Corona's voice broke the tension, pleading and urgent.

"Don't kill me, don't kill me! We can both be saved. I saw a car coming this way!" she cried.

Her words were a lifeline thrown into the abyss, a tantalizing possibility of salvation. Yet, the desert's lessons on trust and deception echoed in my mind, urging caution.

My throat was parched beyond words, but desperation forced a hoarse shout from my lips: "You can't fool me!"

Corona, sprawled on the sand, insisted, "Really, a car! A car! It's a car!"

It was true. A medium-sized jeep was barreling towards us, raising a plume of dust in its wake. Relief flooded through me as I realized help was finally here. The vehicle skidded to a stop, and two people leaped out, their eyes wide with urgency.

"I'm Ash Morris," I croaked, my voice barely a whisper. "Are you here to find me?"

"Yes, God, we finally found you!" they exclaimed, their relief mirroring mine.

Corona and I, united in our desperation, begged for water. "Water, for God's sake, bring water!" we cried in unison.

Two canteens were thrust into our hands. We drank greedily, the water reviving us, though it stung my cracked lips.

Once my thirst was slaked, I pointed to Corona, my voice steadier. "She is the leader of the robbers. Take her to the local police station."

They quickly apprehended Corona, leading her to the vehicle. I clambered in after them, exhaustion pulling at the edges of my consciousness. The jeep roared to life, slicing through the desert for an entire day, bypassing several oases without pause. As evening fell, we arrived at Yali Oasis.

There, I reunited with Flora and Mateo.

I thrust Corona toward Mateo, my voice cutting through the tense air. "Look at her," I proclaimed, "the very person you've been seeking!"

But before I could witness his reaction, exhaustion claimed me, pulling me into an abyss of darkness. My body, finally overwhelmed by the ordeal, surrendered completely.

In the sanctuary of Yali Oasis, I found solace and care. Over the next two days, my battered body slowly healed, tended by compassionate hands. Meanwhile, justice descended swiftly upon Corona—her execution a stark and final act. Yet, Mateo remained transfixed by her photograph, an image of gentleness and beauty—

an illusion that belied the harsh reality of her cruel nature.

The divide between appearance and reality was striking, a poignant reminder of the façades we all construct. Corona was not alone in her duality; we all harbor hidden depths and complexities. In our relentless pursuit of survival and identity, we craft masks that often obscure the raw truths of who we are beneath.

Isn't it fascinating? This dance between perception and reality, this intricate web of identity we weave.